The Valentine Veilleux Mysteries

Table of Contents

Valentine Veilleux Mysteries

Kathy Lynn Emerson

writing as

Kaitlyn Dunnett

Introduction

The character of Valentine Veilleux, traveling calendar photographer, first appeared in *The Scottie Barked at Midnight*, the ninth entry in my Liss MacCrimmon Mysteries. She reappeared in the second book in my Deadly Edits Mysteries, *Clause & Effect*. Both series were written under the pseudonym Kaitlyn Dunnett.

"Calendar Gal" and "Death in the Dealer Room" were previously published in my collection of short stories, *Different Times, Different Crimes* (2017). "Murder Out of Focus" and the novella, *A Shot in the Darkroom*, appear for the first time in this volume.

Valentine is one of my favorites among the many characters I've created and I hope you will enjoy reading this complete collection of her sleuthing adventures.

Calendar Gal

I'd barely made it to the outskirts of the city when a police cruiser appeared in my rear view mirror, signaling for me to pull over. My grandfather, George Valentine, who served as the constable of a one-horse town for most of his life, taught me to always cooperate with officers of the law. As soon as I had my RV in park, I fished out my license and registration, lowered the driver's side window, and pasted a polite smile on my face.

"Good afternoon, Officer. Is something wrong?"

"Valentine Veilleux?" he asked.

I blinked at him in surprise. "Either you have extremely good vision," I said, gesturing with the license in my hand, "or I'm more famous than I realized."

I avoided mentioning the third choice, that he'd been looking for me. As far as I knew, I hadn't broken any laws. I travel a good deal—it's the nature of my business—but I'm always careful about things like speed limits and parking permits. When he didn't respond to my quip, my thoughts leapt at once to the worst-case scenario, that something had happened to my parents. They were the only family I had left. Granddad had been gone for nearly five years.

"You need to return to the Westside Country Club, Ms. Veilleux." The officer hadn't yet mastered the experienced cop's stone face. He appeared to be younger than I am, and I'm barely twenty-eight.

"Do you mind telling me why?"

I'd finished the photo shoot the day before. This morning I'd given the proofs to the president of the Westside Wives' Club and headed out. My next job didn't start for two weeks but it was six states away. My plan was to travel via the scenic route, taking pictures for pleasure along the way.

"The detectives have a few questions for you, Ms. Veilleux. Looks like you may have been the last person to talk to Dotty Kinsale before she was murdered."

Well, that was a shocker!

I turned the RV around and drove back the way I'd come, the cruiser following close behind in case I tried to make a run for it. Despite that constant presence in my rearview mirror, I told myself they couldn't possibly suspect me of killing Dotty. It sounded as if I'd had opportunity, but I barely knew the woman. Where was the motive? That being the case, I figured they wanted to know if I'd seen anyone suspicious hanging around when I left the still-very-much-alive victim. I didn't think I had, but I was willing to help the investigation in any way I could.

My positive attitude lasted about five seconds after Detective Frank Crispin walked into the board room at the country club. I'd been sitting at the long table, twiddling my thumbs, for over an hour. I hadn't been alone. The police were using this space as a base of operations near the crime scene. I might have found that interesting, except that everyone treated me like a plague carrier. No one spoke to me beyond telling me to take a seat at the far end of the boardroom table and stay put until the detective had time for me. You'd think I'd at least be offered a cup of coffee! I got it that they were busy, but that didn't explain the suspicious glances officers shot my way when they thought I wasn't looking.

Detective Crispin flashed a badge and ID at me as he introduced himself, the movement so fast that I couldn't possibly see what department he was with or confirm his name. Setting a stack of file folders on the table, he dropped heavily into the chair opposite me.

"You met with Dorothy Kinsale this morning at nine. Is that correct?"

"Yes, it is." It was still hard for me to believe she was dead. I didn't know her well, but she was one of those vibrant women who never seemed to slow down, let alone stop.

"Why?" He managed to make that one word sound like an accusation.

I forced a smile. "She hired me to do a photo shoot for a fundraiser the Westside Wives' Club is planning. Ms. Kinsale is . . . was the president of that group. We met so I could give her the proof sheets to distribute to the other women who posed for me."

"Describe your meeting." He snapped out the command like a drill sergeant trying to scare a recruit.

I managed not to roll my eyes. "There's not much to tell. We met in the members' café. She treated me to breakfast. We talked about the usual things you talk about when you don't know someone well—the weather, the high price of gas, where I was headed next."

Picturing Dotty Kinsale as she'd been only a few hours earlier made me sad. For all her energy, she hadn't accomplished much. As far as I could see, she and the other wives led a rather shallow existence in the shadow of their successful husbands. They might have done a great deal of good with a fundraising effort for some worthy cause, but their idea was to sell the calendars to raise money to plant flowerbeds on the country club golf course, a scheme the club members were apparently willing to approve but not pay for.

"Did she say what she was planning to do next?"

"She was dressed for tennis. I assumed she had a game scheduled." I didn't mention thinking that if I were planning a sweaty activity, I sure wouldn't spent an hour fussing with hair and makeup. But that's just me. I don't fuss much in any case.

"Was she worried? Upset? Nervous?"

"She seemed to be in a very good mood. Pleased with herself." And like a good trophy wife, she'd only picked at her food, although she had filched a slice of my bacon.

He pulled a folder from the stack beside him and slapped it down in front of me. "You want to tell me what these are?"

Since the folder sported my business logo, an old fashioned camera from the 1890s with the words CALENDAR GAL forming a half circle above it, I didn't need to open it to know what was inside. "This contains the page proofs I gave Ms. Kinsale. Each page shows a different woman in four poses. The idea was for each subject to select the pose she liked best. Once they made their decisions, I'd turn the photographs into a calendar—twelve months and a cover. That's how I make my living," I added. "I have a program on my computer that places photos in a calendar format. I send the file to a publisher with an order for the printed calendars and they're shipped direct to the customer."

He opened the folder, revealing Dotty's four poses. "She's naked. All these women are."

"And your point is?"

I shouldn't have tried to be flip. Detective Crispin did not have a sense of humor. At his sour look, I indulged myself with a long-suffering sigh and tried to explain.

"Have you ever seen that old movie, *Calendar Girls*? A group of British clubwomen come up with a gimmick for raising money, a calendar filled with light-hearted photos of ordinary women doing ordinary things, except that they're doing them in the nude. The essentials were covered with flowers, or because the model was seated at a piano, or—the classic—using two enormous muffins to hide a generous bosom. The Westside Wives' Club figured they could rake in a bundle by creating something similar. They hired me to make it happen."

"Is that your area of expertise? Girlie pictures?"

What century was this guy living in? "My area of expertise is *photography*."

"You've never been in front of the camera?"

I rolled my eyes and held onto my temper. I knew what he was seeing—a green-eyed, strawberry blonde in skinny jeans and a turtleneck jersey that had a tendency to cling. You'd think the serious-looking glasses—a necessity, not an affectation—would be enough to counter his first impression, but apparently not.

"I'm not a model. I'm not stacked enough to be a centerfold and I'm only five foot five, much too short for the runway."

He still didn't crack a smile. This was going to be a long afternoon. Reaching for the folder, I flipped through the contents, looking for the best examples to show him. The shots showed a lot of skin, but none was X-rated. If I do say so myself, most were pretty clever, modeled upon but not copies of the calendar photos in the movie. The one I was looking for showed a tall brunette who really did have a centerfold figure. Crossed arms and crossed tennis racquets kept her decent. The mischievous smile on her face should have been enough to make the most hardened cop chuckle.

My fingers froze on the last of the photos as I reached the bottom of the pile. Frowning, I sat up straighter. Where was Miss Tennis Racquets?

"Okay, this is weird." I went through the stack a second time. "There are only nine proof sheets when there should be thirteen. Four sets are missing."

"Whose?" For the first time, Detective Crispin showed a bit of emotion. Unfortunately it was still heavily tinged with suspicion.

I shook my head. "I didn't work with these women long enough to get all their names straight, but the files in my RV are labeled."

"Let's go," he said, standing.

On the way to the RV, we were waylaid by Donald Markey, manager of the Westside Country Club. I hadn't had much to do with him during my shoot, but he'd taken pains to let me know what a huge exception he was making to let me camp out in the parking lot by the Dumpsters. He was one of those reed-thin, meticulous types. He'd have been perfect for the role of an English butler in a romantic comedy. He didn't have the accent, but he'd mastered the art of looking down his nose at the hoi polloi.

"Are you arresting this woman?" he demanded, meaning me.

"On what charge?" I could swear I saw Crispin's lip twitch with amusement, but I must have been mistaken.

Challenged, Markey started to sputter. "It's those photographs she took . . . naked women . . . misuse of country club facilities."

"We're continuing our investigations," Crispin started to push past him, but I dug in my heels.

"Wait a second. Mr. Markey, who told you about the poses for the calendar? It was supposed to be kept under wraps." I winced at the choice of words, but they were the ones Dotty Kinsale had used when she'd sworn everyone to secrecy. She'd told me she wanted the calendar to be a surprise—saving the "big reveal" for the day of the fundraiser.

Markey drew himself up straighter—a good trick when he already looked like he had a ramrod for a spine—and sneered at me. "One of our club members admitted to being tricked into participating in this disgusting travesty."

"Which one?" Crispin was tugging me away, but I twisted in his grip to keep eye contact with the manager.

"That's confidential information."

"I don't think it was one of the wives at all," I muttered as Crispin steered me toward the spot where I'd parked. "I'll bet a caddy, or one of the busboys got an eyeful through a window and just couldn't wait to rat on us to the boss. Markey just doesn't want anyone to think he *allowed* the shoot to go on."

If he'd complained to Dotty, she'd have shut him down fast enough. After all, the manager worked for the members, and Dotty and her fellow clubwomen were among the most influential of those members. *Some people,* I thought as I unlocked the RV, *just like to find fault.*

Detective Crispin let out a low whistle when he saw my setup. With the inheritance my grandfather left me, I had my home-on-wheels customized. In addition to the compact living quarters, my RV features a full computer workstation with a swivel chair. Everything I needed to turn digital photographs into calendars was at my fingertips.

I called up the files for the missing pages and rattled off the names to go with each of them as they came out of the printer. While Crispin was looking them over, I clicked out of one program and into another to check my email. A familiar named popped up—Dotty Kinsale. My fingers shook a little as I opened the message. She'd sent it less than an hour after I gave her the proof pages.

"Huh," I said, attracting Crispin's attention.

"I want a copy of that," he said when he'd read the message over my shoulder.

I was so rattled that I didn't even remember to change the paper in the printer from photo to all-purpose before I hit the print key.

Dotty Kinsale had cancelled her order for 500 copies of the calendar.

Crispin tapped the printout, indicating the time recorded on the email. "This was sent before you left here this morning, right?"

"Looks like it." I was still trying to make sense of the cancellation. "She examined all the photos over breakfast. She seemed delighted with them. I can't imagine what changed her mind."

When Crispin didn't say anything, I swiveled my chair to look at him and found him looming over me. "This mean you're out a lot of money?"

"If you think I knew about this earlier and killed her because she cancelled the contract, you're way off base. First of all, I didn't know about this until just this minute. Second, I'm not out any money. I'm paid a substantial, non-refundable kill fee, in advance."

It was an unfortunate term, given the circumstances. Although I felt certain Crispin had heard of kill fees before, he clutched the photos and the printout of the email more tightly and gave me a hard stare. "They tell me you lived in your RV while you were here."

"That's right. I was given permission to park at the rear of the clubhouse by the service door, out of sight of the members arriving in their Jaguars and BMWs." They had let me use the facilities, though—pool, tennis courts, showers. That had been a nice perk.

Crispin's face gave nothing away. After a moment he spewed out the clichéd "Don't leave town" speech and instructed me to pull the RV around back to the same spot I'd used throughout the past week. Promising to clear it with the country club manager, he left, but I knew I hadn't seen the last of him.

I followed orders. Then I sat in the driver's seat staring out at a Dumpster and the golf course beyond. I did not like the idea of being stuck here indefinitely, but it didn't look as if I had much choice in the matter.

With nothing better to do, I returned to my work station and called up the files for the shoot. I'd taken more than four shots per person. The ones I'd given Dotty were just the best of the lot.

My contracts specify that the pictures I take for a particular calendar project belong to the customer, but I keep the files for a year after the job is finished. Sometimes individual subjects want copies of other poses. Sometimes the fundraiser is so successful that they need to reorder, or want a second edition for the following year. Outtakes are great for that. I wondered if the police wanted a complete set. Whether they did or not, I certainly wasn't going to delete anything, not when Detective Crispin looked as if he'd really, really like to pin the crime on a convenient outsider like me.

I hit "slide show" and the images appeared, one by one, each filling the entire screen for a few seconds. As I watched shots of my thirteen subjects scroll past, all of them wealthy, middle-aged women with too much time on their hands, I remembered something one of them had said in passing. The idea for the calendar had been Dotty Kinsale's, but going ahead with the project had required a vote by the entire membership of the Westside Wives' Club. It struck me as odd that Dotty had the authority to cancel it without consulting the others.

She had to have made the decision herself. She hadn't had time to share the proof pages with twelve other women between the time I gave them to her and the time she sent that email. I didn't think she'd had time to share the four missing pages, either, unless those four women had already been at the country club. If they had been, I hadn't seen them. It was a weekday morning and there hadn't been many people around at all. There had been more wait-staff than customers in the café.

The photos started to cycle a second time. I stared hard at each one. I didn't see anything out of the ordinary until one of the rejects flashed onto the screen. It was a shot of Gillian Mortimer, a plump redhead, posing with her golf bag strategically positioned to avoid an X-rating. She had blinked at the wrong moment and been immortalized with her eyes closed, reason enough to reject the image. There was another problem with the shot, but it was one I could have fixed by cropping if everything else had been acceptable. In the background, just visible off to one side, were Gillian's clothing and other possessions, carelessly tossed into a chair.

I stared at that section of the photograph, struck by a detail I'd failed to notice before. With a few clicks, I enlarged the area in question. A woman's hand hovered over Gillian's things. It was holding a phone, one clearly plucked from the top of the pile. Enlarging again showed me that the phone was turned on and that it appeared to be showing a list of numbers, probably the ones Gillian called most often, although at this size the image was blurry.

I printed the image on the screen and took it to Detective Crispin.

"That's Dotty Kinsale holding Gillian Mortimer's phone. I recognize her rings. I think she's looking for a phone number."

"So?"

"So, Gillian's photos were among the ones missing from the folder I gave Dotty. Don't you find that suspicious?"

"I find everything suspicious, Ms. Veilleux."

I went back to my RV.

No more than ten minutes later, Bitsy Hollowell, another of the four women whose photographs had disappeared, knocked on my door.

"I'm so glad I caught you," she burbled. "We were afraid you'd gone on to your next job."

"The police want me to stick around," I told her.

Her eyes went wide, stretching the limits of her last facelift. "Ooh! Does that mean you saw something when you met with Dotty?"

"Not that I know of. What can I do for you Ms. Hollowell."

"I *told* you. Call me Bitsy. We're all friends here, especially after those photo sessions." She gave a schoolgirl giggle that was a bad fit for a woman of fifty-something. "Well, as you know, I'm vice-president of the Westside Wives' Club. That is, I was vice-president and now I'm president and as soon as I heard about Dotty I made it my business to get in touch with everyone else who posed for the calendar. We took a vote. We want you to turn it into a memorial to Dotty. Put her picture on the cover."

It was obvious Bitsy had no idea that Dotty had cancelled the contract. And apparently neither she nor any of the other wives found the idea of featuring a semi-nude photo of a dead woman to be in bad taste. A compulsive chatterbox, she didn't give me a chance to say a word before launching into a detailed account of her interview with the police.

"They're talking to *everyone*," she confided, "and asking the most intrusive questions. Why, they even wanted to know what our husbands thought of the calendar. As if we needed their permission to pose!"

When she finally left, I made myself a nice hot cup of honey and lemon tea. If I'd been in the habit of imbibing alcohol, I'd have treated myself to something stronger. It had been that kind of day. Sipping the soothing beverage, I drifted back to my computer work station. Bitsy's babbling, together with that photo of Dotty holding Gillian's phone, had started me thinking. What if there were one or two husbands who *would* object to their wives appearing semi-nude on a calendar?

Then I took my what-if a step further: what if Dotty had been counting on objections?

Blackmail is a nasty business. It can get a person killed. I wondered if the police were thinking along the same lines. They weren't going to tell me about it if they were, but since I was stuck here, I had time on my hands. I took another sip of tea, limbered up my fingers, and clicked on the icon for my favorite search engine.

The husbands of the four women whose photos had gone missing—Gillian Mortimer, Bitsy Hallowell, Doreen Seckler, aka "Miss Tennis Racquets," and Alison Whittier—were all high-profile businessmen, but that didn't necessarily mean they'd consider the photos a problem. Despite Detective Crispin's snide comments, there was nothing pornographic about the pictures I'd taken. Adjectives like "funny" and "cute" and even "silly" applied while "risqué," let alone "dirty," did not. My subjects bared more flesh at the country club swimming pool and, considering what was posted every day on social media, and the craze for selfies that shared way too much, I didn't see how anything in the Westside Wives' Club calendar would be considered the least bit offensive.

But that was me. I had no way of knowing the dynamics of any of these women's marriages. Then, too, if one of the husbands worked for a company that had no sense of humor about such things, that might make him pretty desperate to suppress the evidence. Was that what Dotty had been counting on?

The more I thought about it, the more sense it made. She'd suggested the calendar. After she had the blackmail photos in her hands, she'd lost no time cancelling the project. Then she'd met one of her intended victims and it hadn't gone quite the way she'd planned.

I hadn't been told where she'd been murdered, but I assumed she'd still been at the country club, since the police were set up here. Had she kept her tennis date? Who had her opponent been? Where had her body been found?

I opened a text file and started typing in questions. I had plenty of them, but very few answers. I was staring at the list when someone else rapped on the door of the RV. I barely had time to exit the program before it opened and a tall, burly man I'd never seen before stepped inside. He was dressed in a well-tailored suit, but my first thought was that he looked like a thug. His nose had been broken at least once. His hands were enormous.

"Excuse me," I said, scrambling to my feet and wondering if anyone would hear me if I screamed. "Do I know you?"

"Ms. Veilleux?" His voice was low and menacing.

"Who wants to know? If you're a cop, I want to see some ID" There was another exit, next to the driver's seat, but I'd have to do some fancy maneuvering to reach it before he could grab me.

He chuckled. "I'm not a cop."

When in doubt, lie. "Well, just so you know, one should be here any minute. Detective Crispin just called to say he was sending someone to talk to me."

"Then we'd better finish our business before he gets here."

I backpedaled and ran straight into my desk chair, landing in the seat with an undignified plop when the edge of it caught me on the back of my knees.

"You took pictures of my wife." The man didn't come any closer, but I felt the menace in him all the same. "I want them. All of them. All the copies. You will not use them in a calendar or anywhere else."

I didn't think telling him that all the wives had signed a release form would mollify him. I swiveled to face the monitor and held my fingers poised above the keyboard. "You'll have to tell me her name."

"Joanna Chandler."

I had to call up her pictures to remember which one she was—the mousy little women who hadn't said two words the whole time I'd been taking pictures. I'd had the sense at the time that the other women had bullied her into posing. I felt her husband lean closer as her image filled the screen. It showed her standing behind an archery target. What showed? Her head, her bare arms, and one bare foot.

"Oh, for the love of Mike," Chandler muttered.

The rest of Joanna's pictures appeared on the screen, one after another. At the second, my visitor made a snorting sound. At the next, it turned into a chuckle. By the time the sequence came to an end and I turned to stare at him, his amusement had evolved into a full-on belly laugh and there were tears rolling down his cheeks.

"Forget it," he said when he was able to speak again. "I was going to pay you to suppress the pictures, but they're priceless."

"You're not worried about other people seeing them?"

"I never was. It's Joanna who's embarrassed. She insisted I come here and convince you to destroy them. Me, I think the exposure will do her good. She needs to come out of her shell."

Since I'm not a therapist, I kept my opinion to myself. Mr. Chandler was still chuckling as he left.

I sat back and considered. Just because one husband thought the calendar was a good idea, didn't mean they all did. I got up and locked the door.

I had to unlock it again a few minutes later when a police officer sent by Detective Crispin really did show up. You'd better believe I checked his ID

He took me through the same questions Crispin had asked me. I gave the same answers. Then I tried again to suggest that the murderer might be one of the husbands of the four women whose pictures were missing. I told him about my visit from Mr. Chandler, figuring the police ought to check him out, too, just to be safe.

"Don't you think it's more likely Ms. Kinsale took those pictures out of the folder herself?" the officer asked. "Maybe she didn't like them. Maybe that's why she canceled your contract."

I stared at him. Did he really believe that, or was he just trying to get a rise out of me? I had the uncomfortable feeling that I wasn't entirely off the hook as a suspect.

"What I think is likely is that the murderer removed the pictures. Maybe Dotty had already separated them from the rest because she hoped to blackmail those husbands, but even if she didn't, taking more than one set of photographs would confuse the issue. If he took only his own wife's pictures, that would make him the obvious suspect."

This made perfect sense to me, but the officer was shaking his head. "Amateurs," he muttered as he headed for the door.

Did that mean those four men had alibis? Or that the police had another suspect in mind? I still didn't know who Dotty had been planning to play tennis with. Maybe her opponent had been a sore loser.

Now I *was* getting fanciful. I wished they'd let me leave. As long as I was stuck here, my mind kept circling back to the murder, wondering and worrying. Yes, worrying. It hadn't escaped my notice that the killer might know I had copies of his wife's photos. What was to stop him from coming after them?

I told myself not to be ridiculous. If Dolly's murderer knew that much, then surely he realized that I'd already given copies to the police. All the same, I didn't sleep well that night.

The next day Detective Crispin re-interviewed me. Same questions. Same answers. Except that this time he also asked me about my visit from Mr. Chandler. I recounted the conversation. He told me zip. Nada. Nothing.

A little later, chatterbox Bitsy stopped by again, all aflutter to tell me that Joanna Chandler had stood up to both her husband and the other women in the club and refused to allow her pictures to be used on the calendar. The project was to go ahead, but since they were now short one model, Bitsy wanted me to use two shots of Dotty, one on the cover and one for June, the month Joanna had been assigned.

I reminded myself that the customer is always right and spent the next two hours with Bitsy hanging over my shoulder while I set up the pages. Once they were approved, a click of a key sent the calendar file off to the publisher. Bitsy clapped her hands together and bounced up and down like a three-year-old at a birthday party.

"I'm so glad the police made you stay," she blurted.

"Have they talked to you again?" I asked.

She giggled. "They interrogated *everyone*. All the staff, including that stuffy Donald Markey, and all of us *and* our husbands. So silly. Gillian Mortimer's husband made a huge fuss. He didn't understand what Dotty was trying to do."

I came to attention at the mention of Gillian, remembering Dotty's hands holding her phone and looking at her contacts list.

"I'm sure Dotty was just trying to get a jump on the fundraiser," Bitsy went on, " but *he* thought she was asking him for money to leave Gillian out of the calendar. Can you imagine? Dotty would never stoop to blackmail."

"Did he pay her?"

"Of course not. He told my husband that the very idea she'd think she could get money out of him—everyone knows how tight-fisted he is— made his blood boil."

"So he lost his temper with her?" I leaned toward her eagerly, thinking I was about to hear evidence of rage leading to murder.

"He told her to publish and be damned and slammed the phone down hard enough to give her an earache." Oblivious to the obvious, Bitsy rambled on. With a little coaxing, she revealed that Mortimer, Seckler, Hollowell and Whittier—the husbands of the four women whose photos had gone missing—had alibis for the time of Dotty's murder. Mortimer, a banker, had been in his office when he took Dotty's phone call and hadn't left the premises afterward. Seckler was a lawyer who'd been in court at the time. Bitsy's husband, an architect, had been in a meeting with clients. AlisonWhittier was married to a college professor. He'd been teaching a class.

No wonder Detective Crispin didn't give any credence to my theory!

"Did anyone else kick up a fuss about accounting for their whereabouts?" I asked.

"Only the club manager, but he fusses about *everything*. I don't know why his nose was out of joint. The day Dotty was killed, he spent the whole morning way over on the far side of the golf course."

"How do you know that?" I asked.

"He was telling anyone who'd listen, and making sure we all knew that one of the groundskeepers could vouch for him. Paranoid much?"

In my opinion, being a suspect in a murder investigation would make anyone nervous, no matter how innocent they were. If I'd had someone to give me an alibi, I'd have been talking it up, too.

After Bitsy left, I moped. It wasn't that I thought I was any great shakes as an amateur detective, but it had made so much sense to me that one of those four husbands was the killer. Now that they'd all been ruled out, who was left?

I still didn't know who Dotty's intended tennis opponent was. Rather than sit in my RV and brood, I decided to go inside the country club and ask around. What harm could it do? I was just satisfying my curiosity.

Out of habit, I picked up one of my cameras on the the way out, slinging the strap over one shoulder as I went. In the same way some women never leave home without a purse, I feel undressed if I'm not carrying something with which I can shoot pictures.

I checked the café first, hoping to spot one of the wives. I didn't recognize anyone there, not even the wait-staff. Too late, I wished I'd thought to toss my tennis question at Bitsy while I had the chance.

Discouraged, I followed the same route I'd taken after having breakfast with Dotty Kinsale. As I walked down the long corridor that would eventually exit into the lot where I'd parked my RV, I passed several closed doors, one of them with the word MANAGER emblazoned on it in bold letters. At that point, I speeded up, having no desire to encounter Donald Markey. Intent on escape, I almost missed spotting the remnants of crime scene tape on a nearby doorframe.

I'd gone a few steps beyond before I stopped. Something nagged at my memory. I turned back and tried the door to the room where Dotty, apparently, had been killed. It turned out to be a meeting room, furnished in a fashion similar to the boardroom the police were using as their base of operations but much smaller. The conference table was round with only four chairs pulled up to it but that wasn't what caught my attention. It was the open space in front of the door where a section of the wall-to-wall carpet, large enough for a body to lie upon it, had been removed.

I backed out twice as fast as I'd entered and nearly collided with Donald Markey.

"What do you think you're doing? You've got no business snooping around in there."

In the ordinary way of things, I'd have stammered an apology and beat feet.

Instead, I was too stunned to move.

This was not the first time I had seen that fierce, angry expression on Donald Markey's face. I'd been right to think I'd forgotten something. The elusive detail I'd been trying to recall was standing right in front of me, blocking my escape.

When I left the café on the day Dotty was murdered, Donald Markey had been lurking just outside. He'd paid no attention to me. He'd been too intent on glaring at someone who was still inside.

He had not been on the far side of the golf course.

The pieces of the puzzle thudded into place. Markey had been lying in wait for Dotty. He'd been angry about the photo shoot. One of them had suggested that they step into the small meeting room to discuss the matter. Then, somehow, a quarrel had escalated into murder.

I didn't have a shred of proof, but the conclusion I'd jumped to must have shown in my expression. Markey blanched. Then he lunged at me.

I don't remember slipping the camera strap off my shoulder but the next thing I knew, Markey was on the floor, holding one hand to the spot on his forehead where my favorite digital camera had struck him. Hard. He stared up at me, glassy-eyed. I doubted he could stand up under his own power, let alone chase me, but I wasn't about to take any chances. As I fled toward the board room, I screamed bloody murder.

An hour or so later, after I'd given my statement to the police, Detective Crispin actually cracked a smile. It seems he'd had his suspicions of the club's manager all along. The groundskeeper who'd been his alibi was in desperate need of money to make overdue mortgage payments before the bank foreclosed on his house, but Crispin had been unable to unearth any proof that Markey had offered him a bribe.

My testimony, proving that Markey had been inside the clubhouse at a time when he claimed he was elsewhere, was exactly what the police needed to make an arrest. In the end, he confessed. I've heard he's going with the temporary insanity defense. It might even work, since his reason for killing Dotty Kinsale was his offended sense of propriety. He went berserk and killed her because she'd used *his* country club as a backdrop for a "tawdry" photo shoot.

Despite the notoriety surrounding the case, the Westside Wives' Club Memorial Calendar was an enormous hit. The first printing sold out and they ordered another 500 copies, raising more than enough money to plant their flowerbeds. Bitsy assured me she'd be recommending me to all her friends.

My own feelings are mixed. I can't help but think that if I'd passed on the job, Dotty Kinsale might still be alive. It doesn't help to tell myself that she'd have had no difficulty finding another photographer.

The upshot is that, for the foreseeable future, I intend to concentrate on calendars that feature gardens. Or flower arrangements. Pets are okay, too. It's just shooting people that's more trouble than it's worth.

Death in the Dealer Room

"We're going to make a killing with these calendars!"

Laurie Brubaker's cheerful greeting made me smile. She'd been waiting for me just outside the hotel's Sunrise Room, where booksellers and other dealers were displaying their wares, and Laurie's organization, a local chapter of Sisters in Crime, had set up a table to distribute literature, recruit new members, and sell chapter merchandise.

The closed door was guarded by a tall, slender, efficient-looking woman with a clipboard clutched in one capable hand. The bright pink ribbon attached to her name badge marked her as a volunteer. The badge itself identified the event in progress as Murder With A Twist IV.

Laurie, short and plump with curly, snow-white hair, had to tilt her head back to beam at her. "Morning, Darla. This is Valentine Veilleux, the wonderful photographer who shot the pictures for our crime writers calendar. You should have a dealer badge for her. Val, this is Darla Oliver. She's the dealer room coordinator."

Darla gave me a curt nod and busied herself putting a check mark next to my name on the list attached to her clipboard. She glanced at her watch and recorded the time, although I couldn't think why that mattered. She was about to hand me a badge preprinted with my name and a green ribbon that said DEALER in gold letters—apparently it attached with adhesive to the bottom edge of the plastic badge holder—when I stepped back, raised the camera I wore suspended from a strap around my neck, and snapped three quick shots.

"Oh, excellent!" Laurie clapped her hands together in delight. "Val's been authorized to take candid pictures today," she explained to a scowling Darla. "If you want a print for yourself, you can visit her website and purchase it."

Darla looked a trifle taken aback by the suggestion. I didn't blame her. I'd be surprised if I had any takers. On the other hand, it's second nature to me to take pictures everywhere I go. The oddity of the day was my being at a mystery fan convention.

I was a novice when it came to conferences or conventions of any sort but I wasn't at this one to attend any of the panels or workshops. I'd come for the middle day of three because Laurie had convinced me that helping to sell the calendars I'd created and participating in a group signing with some of my models would be a great opportunity for self-promotion. She'd assured me that among the mystery fans attending Murder With A Twist, I was certain to find a few potential clients.

The four hundred or so attendees were billed as "fans who like a little something extra in their crime novels." That "something extra" could range from a paranormal element to humor to hot and heavy romance to futuristic settings to scenes that jumped from past to present. Apparently, the variations are limitless.

I first met Laurie, the current president of her SinC chapter, six months earlier. She hired me to help twelve local crime writers recreate scenes from their forthcoming novels. I was fortunate in that I was able to match almost all of them with their month of publication. In cases where two or more books were scheduled to be released at the same time, the conflict had been resolved with the toss of a coin, but no one had ended up more than a month away from a release date, and every new book was listed in the date square for that day.

I never realized until I shot that calendar that almost all publication dates fall on Tuesday. I compensated by making the Tuesday squares a little larger than those for the other days of the week. Digitally designed calendars are remarkably flexible and I have a good deal of experience in manipulating them. I make my living doing custom photography for calendars, producing a unique product for each client. Most of them are groups who want to sell the result as part of a fundraising or promotional effort.

As soon as I attached my dealer ribbon and pinned the name badge to my lapel, Laurie and I entered the dealer room. With only forty-five minutes to go before the first registered attendees were allowed in, most of the people already inside were busily rearranging stock on six-foot-long tables or setting up their cash boxes and charge machines.

"Our table is at the far end of the room," Laurie said. "Why don't I head on down and take care of the final preparations while you have a look around. Go ahead and browse. There's a nice mix of merchandise here. Be sure to introduce yourself to everyone, too. I've already spread the word about what great work you do."

Snapping more pictures as I went, I followed her suggestion. The bookseller, a corpulent gentleman who, for sheer bulk, could give Nero Wolfe a run for his money, had the best location. His tables were situated right in front of the entrance and took up that entire end of the room. Somehow, that didn't surprise me. The sign on a stand outside the door hadn't read DEALER ROOM. It had boldly announced that this was the way to the BOOK ROOM.

I spotted novels by a number of authors I'd read, although they were writers who were usually shelved in genres other than mystery. Intrigued, I promised myself I'd return to take a closer look before I left for the day.

As I turned to face the end of the room where Laurie had set up shop, the first set of tables to my right offered vintage clothing and T-shirts with slogans on the front. That struck me as an odd combination, but did seem in keeping with this convention. The dealer wore a button that read "My name is Jolene" and she was delighted to have me take a picture of her display.

"Just be sure to mention the name of the shop," she chirped, passing me a business card that identified her as the owner of T-Shirts and Treasures.

Next on that side came two tables occupied by a small publisher with the unlikely name of Woo-Woo Press. Dozens of their books were on display—novels, short story anthologies, and even cookbooks. The man in charge didn't look up from his cellphone as I passed.

I moved on to the venue of a costume shop. An ornately lettered sign offered to supply everything anyone would ever need to dress like his or her favorite fictional detective. To advertise her wares, the proprietor was outfitted as a dowdy older lady complete with knitting.

"Miss Marple, I presume?"

She agreed that she was, and when I introduced myself she made complimentary noises about my photography. Laurie had not been exaggerating when she'd said she'd been talking me up.

Crossing the center space, I backtracked to the first table to the left of the entrance. This dealer, a scarecrow of a man with thinning hair and tinted glasses, had almost as many tables as the bookseller. He specialized in items relating to mystery movies and TV shows. His stock ran to expensive DVD sets, action figures, and an assortment of other collectibles. If the sheer number of items on a single theme was any guide, he was a big fan of Benedict Cumberbatch's Sherlock Holmes.

The last two tables on that side were still covered with dust cloths. Laurie's was just beyond, one of two displays across the far end of the dealer room. The other offered jewelry for sale—gorgeous, one-of-a-kind necklaces, bracelets, and brooches. The proprietor stood in the open space in front of her tables, deep in conversation with the skinny guy who sold DVDs. She was almost as tall as he was, but much more sturdily built. She was also annoyed.

"It's either Calista or a poltergeist," she said. "All the rings on my ring stands are out of order. And there's a funky smell around my tables, too. I had to dig out the air freshener."

"The rings could have been rearranged by one of yesterday's customers. Maybe you just didn't notice until today."

"I like my theory better." The snarky note in her voice intensified when she added, "Do you think she's going to bother to show up today?"

"She'll be here." The expression on DVD guy's face said he wished it were otherwise.

I took their photograph just before he returned to his tables.

The jewelry seller turned an inquisitive look my way. "You must be Val. Nice work on the calendar. I'm Marianne."

"Thanks." I hesitated, then gave in to curiosity. "I know it's none of my business, but who is this Calista you were talking about?"

"She's our absent dealer." Marianne waved one hand toward the cloth-draped tables.

"What does she sell?"

Marianne snorted. "Cat crap." She laughed in a good-humored way at my expression. "Someone once told Calista that cats are popular with mystery readers, so she stocks every hokey cat item you can imagine. Some of them are so cutesy they make you want to barf."

"Nothing but cat . . . kitsch?" The mind boggled.

"Pretty much, although she tries other things from time to time." Marianne straightened a tray of earrings as she spoke. "Once it was stuffed animals dressed up as characters from books, not that you could figure out who they were supposed to be. Then another time she got it into her head that she could sell designer teddy bears. Decades ago, those were a hot collectible. People paid as much as five hundred dollars for a handmade one, but not today, and not at a gathering like this one. The woman is clueless."

"What was that about rings being out of order?" I took a couple of candid shots of Marianne and her tables while she decided whether or not to answer my nosy question. After a moment, she shrugged.

"She's been known to mess with other dealers' displays. Last year Calista and I were both offering cat jewelry for sale. My pieces were better quality. After we set up but before the convention started, they mysteriously disappeared. Then, when we were packing up to go home, they miraculously turned up again."

"And the DVD guy? Has he had trouble with her, too?"

"Norman. Yes. Two years ago, he had some collectible or other with cats on it. Different year. Same story."

"This is Murder With A Twist number four," I observed. "Did anything happen three years ago?"

Marianne frowned. "You know, now that I think about it, it did. To Calista. She claimed some of her stock was stolen from the dealer room. Made a big stink about it, too. But the kicker is that nothing was missing at all. Turned out she just forgot to load those particular boxes into her car. They were sitting in the garage at her house the whole weekend."

At that moment, Laurie caught my eye, gesturing for me to join her. I told Marianne I'd be back later, with my credit card—it really was gorgeous jewelry—and moved on to snap a few pictures of Laurie's display. At its center was a huge stack of calendars. The cover showed all twelve mystery writers wearing the outfits they'd devised for the shoot.

"We did well yesterday," Laurie said as I settled into a not-very-comfortable folding chair, the twin of the one she occupied. "We sold over fifty copies. I expect they'll all be gone by the time we shut up shop on Sunday, especially with the group signing scheduled for this afternoon."

"That's great." All the money raised was going to fund the chapter's grant to a promising unpublished writer.

She glanced at her watch. "Fifteen minutes until Darla opens the door to the thundering herd."

"They'll probably head for the bookseller first." I opened the tote bag I'd brought with me. I left my laptop, a second camera, and several attachments where they were and pulled out a stack of business cards and a handful of flyers showing calendars I'd produced for other clients.

"Hard to say." Laurie shrugged. "Books are good, but lots of folks still need costumes."

"Please tell me this isn't one of those conventions where *everyone* dresses like a favorite fictional character."

She laughed. "Only for the Saturday night banquet, but there's a prize for the best outfit."

I was about to ask for more details when we were interrupted by a hair-raising scream.

A second shrill, ear-splitting cry had me out of the chair and circling the Sisters in Crime table. Marianne, her movements erratic, stumbled through the narrow opening between her tables and Calista's. One hand was clapped over her mouth. The other arm flailed wildly, knocking over the wig stand she used to display a particularly ornate necklace.

The bookseller raced down the length of the room with a speed that belied his girth and caught her by the shoulders. He gave her a single hard shake. "Get a grip, Marianne. What's wrong?"

"She's dead, Alex," Marianne gasped. "Somebody *killed* her."

"Who's dead?"

"Calista. I went to stash an empty box underneath one of my tables and . . . and . . . ." Shoulders heaving as she sobbed, Marianne couldn't go on.

"Maybe she can be revived." Jolene stood beside them, wringing her hands but making no move toward Marianne's tables. "Does anybody know CPR?"

It was left to me to bend down and lift the edge of the floor-length skirt at the front of the middle table.

CPR was not going to help.

A swollen, discolored face looked back at me. Calista was definitely dead. A thin metal wire bit deeply into her neck.

With a choked cry, Jolene backed up so fast that she tripped over her own feet and nearly fell. Norman, the DVD guy, caught her arm to keep her upright. Just as quickly releasing her, he leaned in to take a look at the body for himself.

Still crouched in front of the table, I glanced his way. "Calista?"

He nodded and swallowed convulsively. My stomach was none too steady either. I lowered the table drape and stood.

"Cripes, Marianne," said Alex, who had also gotten a good look at the murdered woman. "What did you want to go and kill her for?"

"I didn't lay a finger on her!"

"She was strangled with a length of your beading wire."

Marianne opened and closed her mouth but nothing came out. Laurie took her arm and steered her behind our table, urging her to sit down while she fished a bottle of water out of the cooler stashed behind the chairs. She'd brought a good supply, along with sandwiches and snacks.

If Marianne is a murderer, I thought, *I'll eat my camera.*

The publisher of Woo-Woo Press held up his cellphone. "I called 911. The police are on their way. They said not to touch anything."

Jolene looked stricken. "That means we can't open."

"Good old Calista," Alex grumbled. "Thanks to her, this weekend is going to be a dead loss for all of us. The cops will turn this whole room into a crime scene."

"It would have been considerate of her to wait until tomorrow to get herself killed," Norman muttered. "We never have as many sales on Sunday as we do on Saturday."

"I hope they don't get fingerprint powder all over my stock," said the pseudo-Miss Marple. "It'll be impossible to remove from the more delicate fabrics."

I looked from one dealer to another but saw not a single sign of grief over Calista's death. They were all much more upset over lost profits. It was a sad commentary on the dead woman's life, but did it also mean that one of them had killed her?

It was at that moment that Darla Oliver opened the double doors at the entrance of the Sunshine Room. She stepped inside, pushing one of them back toward the catch designed to hold it open.

"Stop!" Norman shouted.

With a start of surprise, Darla turned to stare at him.

Once again, Alex, the bookseller, took charge. He blocked the customers on the other side of the door from coming in. I couldn't hear what he told them, but after he'd said his piece, only Darla had joined us in the dealer room.

She kept her clipboard clutched in front of her like a shield while Alex explained the situation. That was her list of dealers, I realized, and Darla had been recording the time each of them arrived.

"Who was here first this morning?" I asked.

Darla had a dazed look on her face and didn't seem to hear the question, but Alex caught my drift. He took the clipboard away from her and scanned the list.

"Calista checked in at seven-forty-five. Then Marianne showed up at eight and Jolene at eight-ten."

"That's not right." Marianne's eyes were wide with shock. "No one was in this room when I got here." She drew in a shaky breath. "Oh, God! Calista's body must have been under the table the whole time I was uncovering my stock and straightening the display. I didn't have any reason to look underneath."

No one mentioned the "funky" smell she'd said she noticed.

"Marianne was the only one here when I arrived," Jolene said.

Abruptly, Darla came back to life. "That's because the other woman was already dead!" She pointed an accusing finger at Marianne. "You killed her! It had to be you. You were the only other person here."

"Someone must already have been in the room when Calista got here," Marianne shot back. "The murderer was lying in wait for her." Then she gasped. "Or waiting for whoever came in first! Oh, God! It could have been me lying there!"

"Impossible," Darla snatched her clipboard back from Alex. "The Sunrise room was *locked* until I got here. As dealer room coordinator, I was the last one out yesterday. I watched while someone from the hotel staff secured the doors. No one was permitted to unlock them again until I arrived this morning and I can assure you that this protocol was followed to the letter."

"You need to notify the board of directors," Alex told her. "Hotel security, too."

Darla cast one last appalled glance toward the table drape hiding the body as she reached into her pocket for a cellphone. She headed for the farthest corner of the room as she punched in a number.

The color started to come back into Marianne's face, but her hands trembled when she took another sip of water. Being accused of murder would make anyone shaky.

"Is there another way in?" I asked.

"Good thinking," Laurie said. "There are service doors." She jerked her head toward the curtain covering the wall behind her. "But they're supposed to be kept locked, too."

Marianne made a strangled sound. "*Supposed* to be."

"Meaning?" I asked.

"At the very first Murder With A Twist, on Sunday morning, we came in to find a woman from the custodial staff vacuuming the floor. She'd already taken out the trash. Nobody had told her she had to wait for the dealer room coordinator, or that she shouldn't use the service corridor behind this room to get in and do her job."

"I wonder how hard it would be to get hold of a key?" Laurie mused.

"Assuming you'd even need one," Jolene chimed in. "I remember this one time, at a different hotel, no one remembered to lock the service doors at all." Propping one broad hip against the Sisters in Crime table, she leaned across it to give Marianne a reassuring pat on the arm. "I know because it was raining that day and the only place I could find to park was closer to the exit from the service corridor than the main entrance. I figured I might as well check that door, just in case I could get in that way and, lo and behold, it was unlocked. I was glad not to get drenched, but kinda ticked off, too. I mean, anyone could have waltzed right into the dealer room and walked out with all our merchandise."

Norman had been listening from a short distance away. Now he ducked behind the curtain. "These service doors are locked," he reported.

"They are now, but what about earlier?" Laurie asked. "No way to tell, right?"

Marianne groaned. "They're locked now. That's all that counts. My wire. My tables. And Darla's clipboard proves I was in here alone with Calista. The police are going to think I killed her."

With a vigorous head shake, Laurie disagreed. "In fifteen minutes? Maybe that's long enough to garrote someone, but it's cutting it awfully close when you'd also have to tidy up afterward."

Everyone stared at her.

"Oh, please. You don't have to be a cold-blooded killer to know how to commit a murder. It's called research. Calista was no lightweight. She wouldn't just stand still and let someone pull a length of beading wire tight around her neck. She'd struggle. Things would get knocked over."

I pointed out the obvious: "She could have been killed in the middle of the room." With no customers, there was plenty of open space.

Laurie was undeterred. "It would also take time to tuck the body out of sight under the table. Kill *and* hide before Jolene showed up? I don't think so." She turned to Marianne, an encouraging smile on her face. "Where do you keep your beading wire?"

"In a box of supplies. When there aren't any customers, I work on new pieces."

"So anyone could have taken it. Oh!" Struck by a thought, she frowned, then grabbed one of Marianne's hands, turning it over and then holding it up for everyone to see. "Look. No cuts. Using that wire as a garrote would have left marks. And that's how we can find the real killer."

I hated to spoil Laurie's theory, but there were ways around that problem. "The murderer probably wore gloves, or wrapped the ends of the wire around something."

"The ring stands," Marianne said in a shaky whisper. "That's why the rings were out of order."

I was still trying to erase that unsettling image from my mind's eye when the police arrived.

They herded us into another room and ordered us not to talk to each other. Since I hate to be idle, I asked the policewoman left to keep an eye on us if it was okay to work on my laptop. After exacting a promise that I would not send any email or post information about the morning's events on social media, the detective in charge gave his permission and I set to work transferring photos from my camera.

On the larger screen, I could see details much more clearly. I wasn't looking for anything in particular, just playing around to pass the time, cropping some photos and enlarging sections of others, when something in one of the pictures I'd taken of Darla caught my attention. She was holding her clipboard so that a section of the top page was visible. Since the shot was enlarged, I was able to read a few of the names on her list, including that of Calista Donahue.

I increased the size again just to be sure, but there was no mistake. Contrary to what Darla had claimed, she had not checked Calista in at seven-forty-five. As late as my arrival, the space next to her name had still been blank. Darla had added the time *after* Laurie and I entered the dealer room.

One by one, dealers had been called out to be interviewed. It was a slow process. Laurie, Jolene, Marianne, and I were still waiting our turn when I made my discovery. I wasn't a cop, or even a mystery writer, but I couldn't help but be curious. I clicked on my favorite search engine and started digging.

By the time I was escorted into a small conference room to talk to a police detective, I was pretty sure I knew what had happened to Calista Donahue. In answer to his questions, I told him what I'd seen and repeated everything I'd overheard in the dealer room. Then he asked me if there was anything else I'd like to add to my statement.

"Yes," I said. "I know who killed her."

He gave me a skeptical look. "Go on."

"Three years ago, Calista Donahue claimed that some of her merchandise was stolen from the dealer room. That was the same year the dealers arrived on Sunday morning to discover a member of the custodial staff already inside. She came in through the service corridor to vacuum and take out the trash. According to what I found online, Calista accused that employee of theft."

The detective began to take notes.

"A newspaper account said a woman named Joyce Graham was arrested. She was also fired from her job at the hotel. I didn't find a follow-up article, but I know there was no case against her. That poor woman was thoroughly traumatized for nothing. Calista found the missing items when she got home. She'd never brought them to the hotel at all." I drew in a shaky breath. "The story doesn't end there. I found Joyce Graham's name in the newspaper a second time just a few weeks later . . . in her obituary. The wording makes me think she committed suicide."

"That's very sad," the detective said, "but how does it connect to Calista Donahue's murder?"

"The obituary listed Joyce Graham's closest relative, a sister. Her name was Darla Oliver."

Suddenly, he was much more interested in my theory.

"I know Darla lied about checking Calista in." I showed him the photograph of the clipboard. My digital file had a time stamp of its own. "It wouldn't have been hard for a room coordinator to get hold of a key to the service doors. Then all she had to do was lure Calista Donahue into the dealer room after everyone else left for the night on Friday. She helped herself to Marianne's beading wire to use as a garrote. Once Calista was dead, she left the body beneath Marianne's tables. It had to have been an afterthought to add the time next to Calista's name—just one more nail in Marianne's coffin. I suppose Darla had heard Marianne mouthing off about Calista—she didn't like her much—and figured she'd make an ideal scapegoat."

"We'll check into it," the detective promised, but I could see he still had his doubts. The way he was shaking his head suggested that he had trouble believing anyone would carry out a simple act of revenge in such a complicated way.

"It was a case of poetic justice," I explained, and was rewarded with a flicker of comprehension.

"Darla wanted Calista to die in the same place where she falsely accused Darla's sister of theft?"

I nodded. "Nowhere else would do. She had to die in the dealer room."

Murder Out of Focus

At the time I agreed to take photographs of Maine's Monday Mountain Ski Resort for a promotional calendar, I hadn't put on a pair of skis for nearly fifteen years. For twelve of those years, I'd been traveling the country in a custom-built RV, billed as Valentine Veilleux, Calendar Gal. My calendars have featured everything from volunteer firefighters to tastefully nude clubwomen, although my specialty is pet photography. When a coffee table book of my best shots of cats and dogs was published, it sold well enough to provide me with a nice little nest egg.

I was looking forward to the fresh air and sunshine, and the resort had agreed to supply me with ski togs and equipment, as well as room and board. A sweet deal all around. A few more gigs like this one and I'd have enough stashed away to buy myself the studio I had my eye on and settle down in one place.

On the first day of my weeklong stay, I was careful not to spend too much time on the slopes. To my relief, I hadn't completely forgotten the skills I learned in high school. The boots, skis, poles, and helmet the resort provided were much more aerodynamic and sophisticated than those I used when I was a teenager. They surpassed the older models in comfort, too, but the real treat was not having to wear multiple layers of heavy clothing underneath a bulky ski parka. The person who developed a lightweight fabric that wicks away moisture deserves a medal.

A long soak in a hot bath before bed soothed away any soreness and I was raring to go on day two. Filled with optimism, I took the lift to the top of the mountain. I intended to ski on a variety of trails, always on the lookout for scenic shots. The view would be ever-changing, since the slopes don't go straight downhill but rather consist of a series of crests and valleys. There are also what are called "glades" where skiers can choose from a variety of routes to pass through wooded areas. I found that concept amusing. The last time I was on skis, going off the open, downhill slopes was strictly verboten.

I thought I was prepared for any contingency, but when I stepped off the chair lift I found myself engulfed in thick fog. So much for taking panoramic shots of the surrounding peaks and valleys. From this height, I should have been able to see all the way to Mount Washington in neighboring New Hampshire. I could barely glimpse my own hand when I held it in front of my face.

The idea of heading downhill into that white mist unnerveded me, but I didn't think it would be particularly dangerous. There weren't many other skiers around, since it's not a lot of fun to ski in foggy conditions. Besides, it was a weekday. I'd just have to take it slow until visibility improved. I told myself that wouldn't take long. Only the very top of the mountain was muffled in a shroud.

I was only partly right. Wispy fog is better than pea soup, but not by much, and it continued to surround me as I descended. I took a few pictures anyway, hoping they might qualify as atmospheric, but I had a feeling they wouldn't be worth saving.

Farther downhill, when the sun finally broke through the gloom, I brought myself to a not-too-awkward halt and unzipped my jacket far enough to free the camera suspended from a strap around my neck. I had just lifted it to frame a photograph of two fellow skiers against the tree line when something large and dark flew past the viewfinder. It passed so close to me that I felt a rush of wind as it went by.

Startled, I shifted my weight and nearly overbalanced. I let the lightweight camera fall to my chest and turned to glare at the person who'd ruined my shot. I expected to see nothing more than the back of another skier, rapidly disappearing down the hill. Instead, the idiot who'd almost bowled me over stopped a couple of dozen yards below me, turned, and headed back uphill.

The maneuver is not one that can be managed with any speed while on skis. I had time to lift my camera and take a couple of photos of the approaching figure before I turned to snap the picture I'd planned to take, albeit with different skiers in the foreground. By the time I looked downhill again, the person who'd come so close to slamming into me was waving a ski pole dangerously close to my face.

I ducked. "Hey, watch what you're doing with that thing!"

It wouldn't have done much damage if it *had* connected. We were both wearing sturdy helmets and industrial-strength goggles. That meant neither of us could see much of the other's face. My hot pink ski jacket rendered me virtually shapeless, but the color probably gave away my gender. My adversary was all in black, right up to and including a ski mask that covered the lower part of the face.

"What the hell were you thinking?" The voice was harsh, but not distinctly male or female. "You don't just stop short without any regard for the skiers behind you."

The unfairness of this accusation left me momentarily speechless. My mouth may have dropped open. If I'd come to a halt just below the crest, where I'd have been difficult to see, I'd have understood the skier's annoyance, but the rule-of-thumb on the slopes is that the person farthest downhill has the right of way. Those uphill, fog or no fog, are responsible for keeping an eye out for others and going around anyone in their path.

"I beg your pardon?" My voice was as icy as the skating pond by the lodge.

My adversary abruptly shoved up a pair of goggles to reveal angry brown eyes and bushy salt-and-pepper eyebrows. "People like you shouldn't be allowed to ski at Monday Mountain."

I could feel my temper rising, but I was brought up to be polite and I'd had plenty of practice dealing with fussy clients. I pressed my lips tightly together to keep from saying anything rude.

My self-control was sorely tested during the tirade that followed. My hands gripped the tops of my ski poles with increasing force as the insults piled up. I particularly resented being compared to careless selfie-takers who tumbled off cliffs while trying to get the perfect shot.

It took every once of willpower to keep from asking: *What is wrong with you?* aloud. I managed only by repeatedly telling myself that even the most vocal of critics eventually ran out of insults, not to mention breath. I watched in morbid fascination as those angry eyes narrowed and focused on my camera.

"You better not have taken my picture. You can't take someone's photo without their permission."

Read the back of your lift ticket, sweetheart, I thought, channeling my inner Humphrey Bogart for the voice. I didn't need my subjects' permission to include them in the pictures I took on this assignment.

Obviously this blowhard had also failed to notice that there were tons of security cameras at Monday Mountain. They were set up all over the ski resort to provide a steady stream of video to the management. They captured images of every single person who made use of the lodges and the lifts. For all I knew, there were a few that covered the slopes as well.

I could easily have argued his point, but it wasn't worth the hassle. I held up my camera, so that the screen was visible and made a production out of finding and deleting the offending shots.

"Satisfied?" I asked.

"I hope you've learned your lesson. You watch your step in the future, young woman." The goggles snapped back into place.

I stayed where I was, more shaken than I wanted to admit, until the obnoxious skier was just a speck in the distance. To calm myself, I began shooting again. With full sunlight now illuminating the scenery and the Presidential Range forming a majestic backdrop, I managed to take some spectacular photographs.

The highlight of the next hour was being accosted by a young couple with skis on their feet and stars in their eyes. Having noticed my camera, they asked me to take their picture.

"We're on our honeymoon," the woman said with a broad smile. "We want to remember every minute of it."

I was happy to oblige, shooting several poses before I added their email address to my phone. I'd send them the digital images as soon as I uploaded them to my computer.

"Twelve of the photographs I'm taking here at Monday Mountain are for a calendar," I told them. "At this point I have no idea which images the owner will choose, but there's always a chance it could be one of these."

"Ooh," the bride squealed. "How exciting."

"I'll attach a waiver for you to sign and sent back to me, just in case."

After my run-in with that nasty skier, I decided it was better to be safe than sorry. Besides, in contrast to most of the other photos I'd taken on the slopes, the faces of my subjects would be recognizable in these.

A short time later, I headed back to the lodge. With luck, there would be a decent-sized crowd gathered around the photogenic stone fireplace, sipping hot chocolate and assorted alcoholic beverages. I'd capture some of that convivial atmosphere before I returned to the workstation in my RV to take a closer look at the results of the day's work.

I was still snapping après-ski pictures when word came that the ski patrol had discovered a body in one of the glades.

SAD AS THAT NEWS WAS, it wasn't something to dwell on. Skiing accidents aren't unheard of, especially if skiers are careless or have an exaggerated idea of their own abilities. In a collision between a skier and a tree, the tree usually wins.

Does that sound cold-hearted? I suppose it does, but since there was nothing I could do to help the poor soul, I retreated to my RV and settled in to earn the substantial fee I was charging for my services.

Instead of the standard dinette found in most campers, mine has a custom-built computer work station where I edit my photographs. The rest of the vehicle is given over to comfortable, if cramped, living quarters. There are, essentially, four rooms. Besides my "office," I have a galley-style kitchen, a bath that squeezes in a shower stall as well as a sink and a toilet, and a bedroom with a queen-size bed. I lack none of the necessities of modern life. The bedroom has a media center and the kitchen boasts a microwave, stove, and refrigerator.

I share my home-on-wheels with a three-legged cat, Lucky, rescued from the side of the road after I saw a car hit her and keep going. Since no one claimed her by the time she recovered from surgery, I ended up adopting her myself.

She curled up on my lap as I worked and didn't so much as twitch when I stopped scrolling through the day's photos to stare at one particular shot. I shoved my glasses back into place a millisecond before they slipped off the end of my nose.

"Huh," I said, squinting. Then I enlarged the section that had caught my eye.

Through the swirling fog, although I didn't realize it at the time, my camera had been aimed at one of the glades. The angle was such that my lens had captured something odd beneath the sheltering trees.

No, I hadn't photographed that unfortunate skier's last moments. Instead, the image on my monitor showed a figure standing in the snow next to one of the trees and reaching up into the branches.

I zeroed in on that spot and increased the size of the image, but the resolution wasn't good enough to show much detail. I could see little more than the back of a dark, bulky form in ski togs. Its hands seemed to be fiddling with something on the side of the tree, but the image was too indistinct to reveal exactly what it was doing.

Slowly, I moved the cursor over the rest of the photograph. To be honest, I didn't expect to discover anything. The distance was too great and wisps of fog kept getting in the way. I had to look twice before I realized what else I'd captured with my camera.

When I did, I made backups of both the photo and the enlarged sections. While 8x10 copies spewed out of my printer, I picked up the phone and called Maggie Pedroia, my contact at the ski resort.

Maggie is co-owner with her husband. Statuesque and generously endowed, with a cheerful disposition, she has a winning way with customers. In the short time I'd known her, she'd pitched in to wait on patrons in the ski shop, serve food in the restaurant, tend bar, and spell the young woman who checked lift tickets—a regular Jill-of-all-trades. I'm pretty sure the idea for a calendar to promote the ski resort had been her brainstorm.

It wasn't until she answered the phone that I realized I wasn't sure what to ask her. Maybe I was wrong about what I thought I'd found. I cleared my throat. "I apologize for bothering you, Maggie. You must be right out straight dealing with that poor skier's death."

"It's a mess," she agreed. "What makes it worse is that he could have been lying there for several hours. The ski patrol regularly sweeps every open trail, but the times vary."

"Could they have saved him if they'd found him earlier?"

"Probably not. He died of a broken neck." There was a long pause. "The state police are here. I'm not sure why. It was an unattended death, but the last time something like this happened, only the sheriff and the medical examiner showed up."

I thought I knew why. "Where are they?" I asked.

"They're working out of a van set up in the parking lot closest to the lodge." Her voice dropped to a whisper. "You were out on the mountain this morning. Did you see anything . . . suspicious?"

Belatedly, it occurred to me that if my photo showed what I thought it did, it might not be a good idea to broadcast that fact. "I was nowhere near any of the glades," I said with complete honesty. Then I ended the call and reached for my jacket and cap. I didn't think it would be hard to spot the van Maggie had mentioned. Unless I was completely off-base, it would be clearly labeled as a mobile crime-scene unit.

FROM A FEW PAST ENCOUNTERS with law enforcement personnel, I know that police officers do not always appreciate offers of help from the general public. The state trooper who finally agreed to talk to me was no exception. He was ready to hustle me out the door the moment I admitted that I hadn't seen the victim, didn't know the victim—not even his name—and hadn't been skiing near the glade where the victim was found.

"But I do have a picture," I said.

"Of the accident?"

Had there been a momentary hesitation before that last word?

"Not exactly." I handed him the manila folder I'd brought with me and watched while he opened it and examined the photographs it held.

"What is this?"

"I think it's someone stretching something between two trees at a height capable of breaking someone's neck if he skied into it. A wire, maybe? Or a thin rope? Not the rope used to cordon off trails. That's too big. Besides, it's bright orange and has plastic flags attached to it."

He stared at me without speaking.

I sighed. "Never mind. I know you can't tell me anything. I hope the photos help."

Since I'd already given him my name and contact information, I left and went back to my RV. Even if I was right, I didn't expect to have any further involvement in the investigation. That was fine with me.

THE NEXT DAY, WHILE having breakfast at the restaurant in the lodge, I read the local newspaper on my iPad. That's how I discovered that I'd crossed paths with the victim before his death. The headshot grinning up at me from his obituary showed a man in the prime of life. He had perfect teeth, artfully styled hair, and an aura of self-importance that no camera could miss.

Skimming the text told me that Marcus Eastman, a lifelong bachelor, had been a mover and shaker in the community for the last twenty years, ever since he inherited a considerable fortune from his late father. If he was "survived by" any other family, they didn't rate a mention.

"More coffee, hon?"

I looked up to find Maggie standing next to me with a carafe.

"Sure." I held out my cup. "Did you know him?" I gestured at the photo.

She shrugged. "More or less."

"I think I saw him in here the other night. He was having dinner with another man."

"That would be Jack Blount. The two of them are . . . *were* the best of friends."

Frowning, I took a sip of my coffee. "Really? I didn't intentionally eavesdrop, but they were sitting at a nearby table and their voices carried. They seemed to be having a difference of opinion."

Not much of a challenge, one had said.

The other had laughed and called his companion a coward.

"I guess you could say they were friendly rivals. It's a toss-up which one of them had a higher opinion of himself." Maggie sent me a rueful smile. "Neither one of them ever tipped more than the minimum."

She glanced around to make sure no one else needed a refill before settling into the chair opposite me and lowering her voice.

"Eastman, he was always difficult to deal with. I'm surprised he had any friends, even a smarmy son-of-a-gun like Jack Blount. I guess they had money and privilege in common, and they were definitely into one-upmanship. Eastman was a braggart. Didn't matter if it was in the office or on the slopes, he always had to prove he could outdo everyone else, especially his best pal." She put air quotes around the last two words.

"So they were competitors?"

"And partners in a real estate business." She gave a disdainful sniff. "Not much better than ambulance chasers, either one of them. You die owning property and you can bet your next of kin will get a phone call within the week." Her gaze shifted. "Speak of the devil."

I turned in time to see a man in a pricey three-piece suit seat himself at a window table.

Maggie scrambled to her feet and hurried over to fill his cup with coffee. "Mr. Blount. How are you doing this morning?"

"As well as can be expected, Maggie." His words carried clearly in the nearly empty restaurant. "It's a terrible tragedy and the police are making matters worse by dragging out their investigation. It's obvious what happened. He ran into a low branch at high speed. Damn fool was always reckless."

Maggie leaned down to fill his coffee cup just as he shifted position to reach for his phone. A few drops of hot liquid landed on his hand.

"Damn it! Watch what you're doing!"

When Maggie attempted to apologize, he rounded on her, turning so that, for the first time, I had a clear view of his face.

Jack Blount was indeed the man I'd seen with Marcus Eastman my first night at the resort, but that wasn't the only time I'd encountered him. Those dark brown eyes and bushy salt-and-pepper eyebrows were unmistakable. Blount was also the blowhard who'd nearly knocked me off my skis.

Since he hadn't spared me a glance and was preoccupied with berating Maggie, I concentrated on finishing my breakfast. I had no desire to renew our acquaintance. Even though I knew it was highly unlikely he'd recognize my face, it was possible he'd remember my pink ski jacket, the one currently draped over the back of my chair. The sooner I was out of his sight, the happier I'd be.

AN HOUR LATER, I WAS back on the slopes. It was a glorious day, cloudless and cold. As I skied down from the top of the mountain, I had a clear view of the glade where Eastman's body had been found. Even without the fog, it was hard to see much detail through the trees, but I thought I caught a glimpse of someone standing stock-still, surveying his surroundings.

As if my skis had a mind of their own, they turned in that direction. A short time later, I found myself confronting the same state trooper I'd spoken to the previous day. The look he shot my way wasn't precisely friendly, but he didn't tell me to go away.

I peered into the bare branches, trying to find the spot I'd captured with my camera.

"Don't strain your eyes. There's no sign of a rope or wire."

"Maybe what I photographed was someone taking it down. If it was wrapped around the tree instead of fastened some other way, there wouldn't be much evidence left behind."

A grunt was his only response.

With a sigh, I resigned myself to having been dismissed. I was about to ski away when he stopped me. "That picture you took. We had it enhanced."

"Did it help?"

"Not much, but your time stamp showed it was taken very close to the time of death. It was a fluke you getting that shot, but it may turn out to be important."

"Is that your way of saying thank you?" I sent a cheeky grin his way and was rewarded with the flicker of a smile.

"You've helped the police before."

I wasn't surprised that he'd checked into my background. "Not by design."

"Word is, you've got sharp eyes and a sharper brain. What do you think happened here?"

"I think someone set a trap for that poor man, then came back and removed the evidence. Were there any tracks by that tree?"

"Dozens. As many skiers as come through here, zipping in and out among the trees, challenging each other to see who makes the best time, it's a wonder they don't have more fatalities."

"Challenging," I repeated, struck by the word.

His eyes narrowed. "Spill it."

I repeated the bit of conversation I'd overheard between Marcus Eastman and Jack Blount. Even before I finished, the trooper was shaking his head.

"Blount wasn't on the mountain yesterday. He had a meeting with a client in his office, and that's a good thirty-minute drive from here."

"Are you sure? Because he nearly ran me down shortly after I took that picture of the glade."

"You saw his face?"

"Only part of it," I admitted. "But I'm sure it was Blount." I gave him a brief description of our encounter.

When I thought about it, it all made a terrible kind of sense. Two longtime rivals into one-upmanship agree to race through the glade. The killer arranges an alibi—an ambulance chaser, Maggie had called him, so not the most ethical sort of person—and sets a trap, challenging the victim to ski into it while he goes around. Once he's sure Eastman is dead, he takes down the wire and, feeling jubilant, races down the mountain to get back to town before his absence is noticed.

"Why confront you if he was anxious to get away?"

"Maybe he was so jazzed by his success that he got reckless. He didn't think it would come back to haunt him because I deleted the photos I took as he was coming toward me. He must have thought that, like most skiers, I was just here for the day and unlikely to recognize anything about him. He wouldn't recognize me, either, not in helmet and goggles."

"It's too bad you deleted those photos."

"They wouldn't have shown much." I considered for a moment. "The resort's security cameras should show him sharing a lift with Mr. Eastman."

"Goggles and helmets," he reminded me, but he looked thoughtful as wished me good skiing and started to make his own way back to the lodge.

"IT'S OPEN," I CALLED when someone knocked on the door of the RV.

Engrossed in cropping a photo on the screen in front of me, I didn't look around to see who'd come in until I heard the door close again behind my visitor. At almost the same moment, Lucky hissed.

It was not a sound she made often and gave me the instant of warning I needed to avoid a blow aimed at my head. Twisting as I turned, I saw a blur as something whooshed past me, millimeters from my face, and crashed into the keyboard.

The desk chair went one way on silent wheels while I flew through the air in the other, grunting when I landed on my side on the carpet. It was only by chance that I didn't knock myself out on my own built-in furniture. Without much room to maneuver, it was another small miracle that I managed to scramble far enough away from my attacker to regain my footing before he could recover his weapon—a length of pipe—and try again.

"What the hell?"

"I don't know how you recognized me, sister, but you aren't going to live to testify at a trial. Without you, they won't have enough to make the charge stick. You're the only one who saw me on the mountain."

"Don't you think the police will be a tad suspicious when they find my body?"

I couldn't believe I'd asked him that, but it wasn't as if I was giving him any new ideas. It was pretty plain he intended to kill me. My only hope was to keep him talking. He was between me and the door, but if someone came by there was a chance we'd be overheard. And if no one did? No matter what, I wasn't about to give up without a fight.

"There won't be enough of you left to tell how you died," Jack Blount said. "These RVs aren't built for winter weather. Easy enough to arrange an accident with the heating. No one will even notice it's on fire until it's much too late to save you."

The scariest thing about him was how calm he sounded. He might have been discussing the weather. Only his eyes gave any hint of the emotions driving him.

Struggling to think clearly through an incipient panic attack, I backed up a few steps. I was almost at the door to my tiny bathroom. If I could get inside and lock it behind me, I'd be trapped, but it would put a temporary barrier between us. I'd be conscious when he started the fire and have a shot of getting out alive.

"Can we talk about this?" I asked. "I don't know why you think I'm a threat to you—"

"Don't play coy with me. You went to the cops. It had to have been you, the one in the pink parka. They hauled me back in, said they knew I'd been on the mountain when my partner died. They bought my alibi until you had to go and blab."

Some of his anger leaked through as he advanced toward me, pipe raised.

He lunged. To evade him, I had to retreat into the bedroom. The backs of my knees connected with the edge of the bed. Arms flailing to keep my balance, my hand came in contact with the ski helmet I'd carelessly tossed onto the dresser. Sheer desperation had me grabbing it up. I flung it in his direction and then, panting, stared in disbelief at his crumpled form.

The helmet had caught him on the side of the head. He was out cold.

He was also blocking the narrow passage that led to the exit.

My foot clipped his chin, making me stumble over his inert form as I fled. I stopped only long enough to scoop up two things on my way out the door—my cellphone and Lucky. I didn't bother with a jacket. By the time I ducked inside the nearest building, the nine-one-one operator had already dispatched officers to the parking lot at Monday Mountain.

AS IT TURNED OUT, THAT thoughtful look I'd noticed on the detective's face had been there because he'd already discovered Blount's season pass had been scanned at the same time as his victim's. They'd ridden the ski lift up the mountain together on the morning Eastman died.

And his alibi? It turned out that Blount had something on the client who'd vouched for him.

The police hadn't needed to see my photo to question Jack Blount again. I just wish they'd told him that. Or, better yet, arrested him before he jumped to the wrong conclusion.

I'm really getting tired of running into criminal types while on the road. It makes buying that photography studio and settling down in one place sound like a much better proposition. After all, how many murders can there be in a small town in rural Maine?

A Shot in the Darkroom

The exterior of the building showed clear signs of neglect. Both the wooden siding and the trim needed scraping and repainting in the worst way and the large upstairs windows, lacking either blinds or shades, looked like empty eyes staring down at the main street of Waycross Springs, Maine. MILLARD'S PHOTOGRAPHY had been painted in gold across the glass of the ground floor display window. Once upon a time, the large letters must have gleamed in the sunlight, but now they were faint and hard to read . Underneath, at half the size but just as worn, were the words WEDDINGS, PORTRAITS, AND PASSPORT PHOTOS. A few lackluster samples of each were displayed in front of velvet—or, more likely, velour—drapes. Their original color, a rich burgundy, was just a memory, but they were intact and shielded the interior of the studio from prying eyes.

A generic FOR SALE BY OWNER sign was propped up in the lower right-hand corner of the window. The phone number at the bottom was written in black Magic Marker, but the notice had been on display for so long that the letters had bleached to gray.

I'd called that number a few hours earlier. Now I was back, discovering that I had to jiggle both the key and the knob in order to persuade the door to open. As soon as it did, I hurried inside and hastily closed it behind me. I didn't expect the interior to be heated, but at least it would be out of the wind. The afternoon was sunny, but it was late February and the temperature hovered somewhere around freezing.

I took several steps into the darkened room before I realized that it wasn't even close to being empty. In fact, it looked as if Aaron Millard had just gone home at the end of the day and never returned.

Although turning on the lights revealed a layer of dust covering everything in sight, I found myself charmed by what I saw. The front of the studio was set up as a waiting area and showroom with a tiny restroom off to one side. Comfortable chairs were grouped around a low, round table on which were piled albums full of sample photographs. There was one for weddings, another for baby pictures, and additional volumes for group portraits, prom photos, and more. I didn't take the time to look through them all, but instead slipped behind the counter with its old-fashioned built-in cash drawer and entered the large, windowless room that occupied the middle of the ground floor.

It appeared that Mr. Millard had taken his cameras with him when he retired, but had abandoned the rest of his photographic equipment. Several lights, each on its own stand, stood ready to illuminate subjects for studio portraits. Backdrops of every description were stacked against one wall. I tested one to verify that the panels were lightweight and easy to shift. There was also an assortment of furniture, mostly decorative chairs and low padded benches. I could visualize a much younger Aaron Millard posing families on one of the latter, telling everyone to say "Cheese" as he snapped a picture to immortalize the moment.

There were two doors at the far end of the long, narrow middle room. One opened into a cramped office containing a desk and several file cabinets. To the far side of the desk, just past an exit into a parking lot, a flight of stairs led upward.

I decided to explore the second floor later. First I needed to see what was behind door number two. Was it too much to hope that Millard had left his darkroom equipment behind? I took a deep breath and went through, flicking on the overhead light as I entered.

My grin must have stretched from ear to ear. Everything a photographer could possibly want in order to develop prints was still there—printer, enlarger, tongs and pans and chemicals, and even a supply of photographic paper. Never mind that hardly anyone uses film anymore. This was a shutterbug's dream come true.

I scarcely felt the cold as I returned to the office and made my way up the stairs to check out the apartment above the studio. In fact, I felt a bit flushed. I could see the layout of the ground floor in my mind. The front room had generous wall space where I could hang prints of my photographs. Part of the middle room could be converted into a classroom and I'd still have enough space left over to take the occasional studio portrait.

Who would have thought that I'd find that prospect appealing? The first job I had as a professional photographer was with a national company that specialized in glamorous head shots. Their clients ranged from actors and writers to anyone—executive, physician, real estate broker—who wanted to plaster his or her face on the wall of an office. Hair styling, makeup, and wardrobe were part of the deal. That wasn't so bad, although some of the getups my clients chose were pretty outlandish. What galled me was that I was expected, at the end of each session, to pressure the customer into ordering a large number of copies of each of multiple poses. Needless to say, the prints weren't cheap, especially if air-brushing was added to the cost.

I stuck it out for two years, but I started saving for what I really wanted to do after week one.

In contrast to the first floor, the upstairs was unfurnished save for some broken and discarded bits and pieces that looked ready for the landfill. I wandered the rooms, taking note of their proportions. There were two ample bedrooms. The kitchen and bathroom were on the small side, but luxurious after what I was accustomed to in the RV. The living room took up the entire front of the building. Its large windows gave a splendid view of the street below and the buildings opposite, with the foothills of Western Maine rising up like a backdrop behind them.

I took up a post on the built-in window seat, curling my legs beneath me, and alternated between studying passing cars and pedestrians and staring at my hands. Was I really going to do this? It wasn't like me to act on impulse. When I'd made plans to go on the road, I'd thought out every angle in advance. I'd spent months just designing my custom RV. Nothing had been left to chance.

And yet this *felt* right.

The advantages were obvious. I was ready to settle down. Without realizing it, I'd been looking for a place to call home for some time. This town, this building, offered a golden opportunity to try different things while still maintaining the career I built for myself.

Think. Consider the disadvantages.

There were plenty of those. For one thing, I didn't know anyone in Waycross Springs.

No, I corrected myself. That wasn't at all true. I'd met Aaron Millard. Despite his crusty exterior, I suspected I might come to like him quite a lot. And the waitress in the restaurant where I'd stopped for lunch—Zillah, her name was—had been happy to tell me all she knew about the business for sale right next door.

I didn't doubt my ability to make new friends in a new place, and although I hadn't asked Mr. Millard how much he wanted for his building, logic told me it wouldn't be a fortune. It was clearly a fixer-upper and Waycross Springs, with its location in rural Maine, nowhere near Portland, or any other city, or the Maine coast, wasn't likely to have sky-high property values.

My income from photographing calendars—it says VALENTINE VEILLEUX, THE CALENDAR GAL on my business cards—had always been more than sufficient to keep me in gas and necessities, but it had been the sale of my coffee-table book of animal photographs that provided me with a substantial nest egg. There had been a nice advance at the start and royalties were still coming in. I'd banked every penny.

Certain I'd be able to afford the purchase price, the only real question was whether or not running a photography studio could be profitable. I'd have to provide a variety of services: classes in digital photography, a gallery of photographs for sale, studio portraits, online sales, and a continuation of my calendar work, only without the constant travel. I'd start work on a second coffee-table book, too.

All of a sudden, panic set in. I *could* do it, but *should* I?

I pulled out my cellphone and punched in a number I knew by heart. I told myself I was thirty-six years old. I didn't *need* parental approval, but I craved it all the same. After two rings, my mother answered.

"Val!" she exclaimed, her delight clearly evident in her voice. "I was just thinking about you."

IT WAS NEARING THE middle of April when I returned to Waycross Springs to finalize the purchase of Millard's Photography. I met Aaron Millard at the local branch of the Carrabassett County Savings Bank, to which I'd already transferred all my accounts.

After careful consideration, I decided it wouldn't be smart to wipe out my entire nest egg. Instead, I made a substantial down payment and took out a modest mortgage for the rest. Despite living the lifestyle of a wanderer, I had a good credit rating. Moreover, I intended to pay off the loan as quickly as possible. I hate the idea of being in debt.

To my mind, a mortgage was only acceptable because I'd need ready cash for repairs and remodeling, but I'd already decided to do as much of the work as possible myself. How hard could it be to scrape flaking paint off a building, brush on primer, and cover the whole with a fresh coat of gleaming white?

Once Aaron Millard agreed to sell me the studio, he insisted I call him by his first name. I met with him several times before leaving the area to complete the calendar shoots I had scheduled. At the bank, he greeted me with his customary gruff formality, standing when I entered the bank manager's office. Scrawny and white-haired, he was probably a few inches taller than my five-feet-five, but at eighty-three he carried himself with shoulders hunched, gnomelike, and tipped his upper body so far forward when he walked that it was a miracle he stayed upright.

"If you'll just sign here, Mr. Millard," the banker said.

Aaron squinted at the documents in front of him, making the deeply incised frown lines around his faded blue eyes and his thin lips appear even more stark under the bright overhead lights in the small, windowless office. For a moment I was afraid he'd changed his mind.

I could understand the natural regret he must feel at letting go of the property that had been at the center of his life for so many years. He was a childless widower who seemed to have spent most of his time for the last few years playing solitaire, reading, and putting together jigsaw puzzles.

He cleared his throat, a habitual sound that was in no way linked to any physical ailment. Slowly, deliberately, he reread the agreement, using one gnarled finger to follow the text. Minute after excruciating minute crept by, until I caught myself clasping my hands together so tightly that my fingernails had left little pockmarks in my skin.

His examination of the paperwork complete, he picked up a pen and scrawled his name on the designated lines. Then he fixed a steely-eyed gaze on the banker. "Got my money ready?"

"Indeed we do, Mr. Millard. And if you'd like to open an account with us, we'd—"

"I'd like it in cash."

The banker's face blanched. "Cash?"

"Greenbacks. Moolah. You *have* heard of it?"

"Yes, of course, but we planned on disbursing the funds with a cashier's check."

"I want the money."

Although he still looked a bit pale, the bank manager took one look at Aaron's stubborn expression and thought better of arguing with him. "It will take a little time, given it's such a large amount. Do you have a preference as to the denomination of the bills?"

"All hundreds will do."

I wondered if Aaron meant to hide the money under his mattress, or maybe in it. I'd realized from the very first time we met that he was a tad eccentric, but this seemed extreme even for him. Thinking I might be able to talk some sense into him, I suggested that we have lunch while we waited for the cash to be readied.

"We could go to Aphrodite's," I suggested. The restaurant was right next door to the photography studio. "My treat."

Aaron wrinkled his nose as if he'd caught a whiff of a bad smell, but then he gave a rusty chuckle. "Why not?"

He was spry enough to get out of the chair without assistance but he walked with a slight limp. Although he carried a cane, he rarely used it for balance and I knew that he regularly walked into town from his house and back again for exercise. I didn't dare offer him my arm.

As old-school as ever, he held the door for me. Once I'd passed through into the lobby of the bank, he turned back to glower at the banker.

"I want my money in an hour. No excuses."

"Of course, Mr. Millard," the banker said, but I thought I heard the sound of teeth grinding together.

AS WE ENTERED APHRODITE'S, I sniffed the air appreciatively. Someone had recently been baking bread. The day's specials, listed on a chalkboard situated beside a bakery case offering a tempting assortment of homemade breads and desserts, included made-to-order, hand-tossed, pizzeria-style pizza, the house specialty, as well as chicken pot pie, quiche Lorraine, vegetarian lasagna, and something called Georgio's Glop.

"What's in the glop?" I asked Zillah Eastlake, the plump, perky waitress who appeared at our table a few moments after we followed the signage that said to seat ourselves.

"Whatever's left over from the day before. Today it's shredded pot roast, baby white and yellow corn, onions, and macaroni in a casserole mixed with tomato sauce, garlic, and herbs and topped with shredded asiago cheese. You don't want to know the calorie count but I can promise you it's yummy, especially when it's nippy out. Guaranteed to warm you right up."

"I'm sure it would."

It would have hit the spot when I visited Waycross Springs back in February, but the mild spring breezes on this day made it comfortably warm. The glop sounded a little heavy, especially when all the portions served at Aphrodite's were generous. I picked up the menu.

By the time Zillah filled two large mugs with coffee, I'd decided on a BLT on rye bread, no mayo, with a side of fries. Aaron ordered the chicken pot pie, then stood up to remove his jacket and drape it over the back of his chair.

That was when I noticed the bruises. Just the edge of one showed above Aaron's loose collar. The other was on his forearm, a deep, purple mark that ran from wrist to elbow and was impossible to miss when he pushed up the sleeves of his sweatshirt.

"What on earth did you do to yourself?" I caught his hand to prevent him from tucking his arm out of sight beneath the table.

"Don't fuss." He pulled in his head, turtle-fashion and refused to meet my eyes.

A reaction that extreme wasn't simple embarrassment. I studied him for a moment before I spoke. "I'm not fussing, but I want to know what happened. Did you fall?"

He gave a snort. "Not without help."

His answer alarmed me, but eliciting details was like persuading a child to give up a toy. A good ten minutes passed before I coaxed him into telling me the whole story.

"Had a break-in at the house a couple of nights ago," he admitted.

"You were *robbed*?"

"Keep your voice down." He glanced around, his expression anxious, but no one in the lunch crowd at Aphrodite's was paying any attention to us. "I wasn't robbed. That scumbag wasn't even successful at burgling me."

Because Zillah was on her way back with a heavily laden tray, I had to wait to continue my interrogation until she'd deposited the food. I goggled at the most generously sized BLT I'd ever been served. The toasted bread was thick cut, the tomatoes and lettuce had been layered with a heavy hand, and a full half dozen slices of crisp, delicious bacon sat on top of them. It was going to be a challenge to get my mouth open wide enough to take the first bite.

Aaron dug into his pot pie with a soup spoon, releasing a puff of steam. Undeterred, he shoveled a huge portion into his mouth, then had to grab his water glass to douse the heat. I waited only until he'd finished drinking before I resumed questioning him, determined to get to the bottom of the situation.

"I'm glad to hear nothing was taken, but that doesn't explain how you were injured."

"Heard someone moving around in the living room in the middle of the night," he said in a gruff voice. "Went downstairs, told him to get the hell out of my house. Got in a couple of licks with my cane before he pushed me down and took off. End of story."

"Hardly! Did you recognize him?" Waycross Springs is a small town, the kind of place where everyone knows everyone else.

"Never got a good look at him." He shrugged. "It was pitch dark. I wouldn't be able to identify him if he walked past me in the street."

"What are the police doing to track him down? Did they find any fingerprints?"

He scoffed at that. "This isn't the big city, Val. Local cops are a useless bunch anyway. Waste of taxpayer dollars if you ask me. Last time the issue came up at town meeting, I voted to let the county handle law enforcement in town. Lost, of course." He shook his head. "The chief of police is the worst of the lot."

"Don't try to distract me with small town politics. Do you have any idea what the thief was after? Why break into *your* house?"

"Who knows?" He lifted his coffee mug using both hands and avoided meeting my eyes. "Drugs, most likely. Everyone thinks old people have medicine cabinets full of the good stuff."

"Yes, but—"

He didn't let me finish. "Hey, Zillah!" he hollered. "Bring me a slice of that double chocolate cake for dessert, will ya? You want one, Val?" he asked. "I don't care much for Henny Horton. She's a nasty old bat, but she sure can bake."

I had yet to meet the infamous Henny, but Zillah had told me she owned Aphrodite's, having inherited the place from her parents.

The excellent appetite Aaron displayed did more than words to convince me that he hadn't been seriously injured. It was clear he didn't want to say more about the break-in, but I couldn't in good conscience let the subject drop completely.

"Considering you had one attempted burglary, do you think it's safe to take all that cash home with you?" I asked.

He winked at me. "Don't you worry about that. I've got plans."

When I tried to press him for details, he politely told me to mind my own business. I wanted to argue, but I gave in and let him change the subject. He was right, and keeping his friendship was important to me.

"You know," I said as we were leaving the restaurant, "just because you sold me the building and everything in it doesn't mean you can't come in and use the darkroom from time to time." He still had all his cameras. I'd seen them stacked in a corner of his living room.

"Might take you up on that. Then again, maybe I'd do better to move with the times and get myself one of them digital cameras." He chuckled. "Hell, maybe I'll even sign up for that course you're planning to offer."

IT WAS A FEW DAYS LATER when I next heard from Aaron Millard. He called at the worst possible moment. On my knees, I fumbled for my cellphone, answering it while trying to finish maneuvering a crumbling cardboard box full of picture frames out from under the counter.

"There's something I need to talk to you about," Aaron said. "Can you come over here now?"

"Not right this minute." I liked the sour old cuss, but his timing stank. I'd hoped to finish getting the front room cleared out before I quit for the day. "Will this evening do?"

"It's important. Something you ought to know. Just in case."

Alerted by the odd note in his voice, somewhere between anxious and querulous, I started to ask what he meant, but he cut me off.

"I'll come to you," he said, and disconnected.

I tucked the phone back into my pocket and returned to rooting around in the dust and cobwebs. I had a major cleaning and sorting job to do before I could put any of my plans for the studio into effect.

I was well aware that there isn't much work for traditional photographers in the twenty-first century, not when every phone and e-reader includes a digital camera. Even passport photos are readily available in any drug- or big box store. I'd been able to support myself for more than a dozen years by focusing on a niche market, taking photographs for specialty calendars, the kind community groups use as fundraisers. I traveled from shoot to shoot in a customized RV that was also my year-round home. Buying a studio and settling down in one place might not have been the smartest move, either professionally or financially, but I thought I had a pretty good business plan.

Since I hadn't been getting as much calendar business as I used to, I hoped that by establishing a physical base, I could diversify. There used to be photography studios all over the place. Camera stores, too. Now it's all electronics. Some people think no one cares about taking a quality photograph anymore. I hope that isn't true, because I plan to offer classes to people interested in taking better pictures with their smart phones and tablets.

Learning a craft is supposed to be popular, especially among retirees. That thought made me smile. According to Aaron, photography is an *art*, not a craft. I think it can be both.

Since I was making steady progress, pausing only occasionally to wipe sweat off my face, I didn't pay much attention to the passage of time. It was only when I heard sirens in the distance that I realized how long it had been since Aaron's phone call. His house wasn't far from downtown Waycross Springs. No two places in the village are. That was one reason the village appealed to me after so many years on the road.

Rising and stretching, I crossed to the display windows at the front and peered out at the street, dusting my hands on the sides of my jeans as I did so. Everything looked as peaceful and calm as ever, but additional sirens had joined the first. Police *and* ambulance? Fire trucks from other municipalities? Something big was going down.

I ducked into the minuscule restroom to wash off the worst of the accumulated dirt and clean smudges off my glasses. After a quick finger comb, I covered most of my strawberry blond hair with a Red Sox cap. I'm not a particular fan, but the wide brim is good for keeping the sun out of my eyes. Since it was a clear, bright day with temperatures near sixty, I didn't bother with a jacket or a sweater, but I did grab one of my cameras. I'd have felt naked without it.

Zillah was standing outside Aphrodite's Restaurant, her nose in the air like a bloodhound searching for a scent. "Don't think it's a fire," she said. "Can't smell smoke."

I wondered how she could tell the difference between the smoke from the wood many local people burned for heat and the flames of a house fire, but I kept that question to myself. "I thought I heard two kinds of siren."

"Police, for sure, and I caught a glimpse of the ambulance just leaving the fire station when I first came outside. Headed north along Church Street."

The fire house was farther east on Main Street, while the police station was off to the west and a block to the south. If the local police had been heading for the same place as the ambulance, they'd probably taken North Road. I hesitated, but only for a moment. Ever since Aaron mentioned that he'd once had a side job taking news photos for the local newspaper, I'd been toying with the idea of making a few extra dollars by offering my work to the local online daily, the weekly *Waycross Springs Gazette*, and any other media outlets that might cover events in the village. This seemed like a golden opportunity to show what I could do.

With a nod to Zillah, I slipped back inside the studio, closed and locked the front door behind me, and walked straight through the building to exit into the municipal parking lot. Since I hadn't yet gotten around to buying a smaller vehicle, my choices of transportation were limited. The RV was way too big to take to the scene of a traffic accident or a house fire. Since the bike secured on its roof had a flat tire, I set off on foot.

I HEADED FOR THE CORNER of the lot adjacent to the intersection of High Street and North Road. From that vantage point, I could see blue lights flashing in the distance. I picked up my pace. Another emergency vehicle, this one the distinctive brown of a sheriff's department cruiser, roared past just as I reached the corner of North Road and Kincaid Street.

By that time I had a pretty good idea where the action was. My heart in my throat, I kept going, closer and closer to the small house Aaron Millard called home.

Neighbors had come out to gawk. I heard bits and pieces of what they were saying as I eased toward the front of the little group.

"Musta been a hit-and-run," someone murmured.

"Probably dead before he hit the tarmac." The voice was high-pitched and sounded more excited than pitying.

"Did anyone see it happen?" a woman asked.

"Don't think so. Terrible thing."

I stopped only when confronted by a man in a blue uniform.

"You can't come any closer, ma'am." He eyed my camera suspiciously.

"Who is it?"

"I can't give you any information, ma'am. Please stay back."

Through the barrier of uniform-clad bodies, I could see the victim's foot. It was clad in the same kind of beat-up athletic shoe Aaron always wore.

"It's Aaron Millard, isn't it?"

Instead of answering me, the officer asked if I'd witnessed the accident.

"No." The word came out on a sob.

"See a car speeding away?"

I shook my head.

He started to turn away, obviously dismissing my value as a source of information.

My vision blurred with tears. "He was on his way to talk to me."

After a brief hesitation, the officer placed a hand on my elbow. "You'd better come over here." He steered me onto the lawn of the nearest house and told me to wait there until someone had time to talk with me.

The moment he released his grip, I started to shake. My legs wobbled. Before they could give out entirely, I folded them beneath me and sat tailor-fashion on the grass, my face buried in my hands. Tears fell hot and fast as I rocked back and forth in a futile attempt to console myself.

I have no idea how much time passed before someone sat down beside me. By then, I'd stopped crying and had shifted position. Keeping my eyes closed, I rested my head on my arms with my hands tightly clasped around my upraised knees. It took an enormous effort to look up and meet the solemn gaze of a different police officer. His nameplate read FLEMING.

"I understand Mr. Millard had an appointment with you."

"That's why he was in the road. He was walking downtown. He doesn't . . . didn't have a car. I should have gone to him, but I was busy and he—"

"Easy." He steadied me with a hand on my forearm. "Take it slow. Why don't you start by telling me your name?"

"Valentine Veilleux."

His dark eyebrows lifted ever so slightly, but that was enough. My shaky grip on my emotions slipped. I jerked free of his grasp and sent a fulminating glare in his direction.

"That is my name." I enunciated every word slowly and clearly. "I'd show you my driver's license if I had it with me, but since I don't, you'll just have to take my word for it."

"Whoa! No need to get upset." His patronizing tone did not calm troubled waters.

"I can tell what you're thinking," I accused him. "Valentine Veilleux would make a good pseudonym for an author of erotic romance novels, or maybe a porn star."

I'd heard both witticisms far too often in my life. I had to admit that my name had a made-up ring to it, but I could hardly change it without upsetting my mother. Valentine was her maiden name and she was very proud of her ancestors.

Sucking in a deep breath, I ordered myself to stop talking. The police wouldn't care if there had been Valentines on the *Mayflower*. Not that there had been. The first Valentine didn't arrive until a couple of decades after the Pilgrims.

"Sorry," I said. "Give me a minute."

He gave me two, then asked, "Why?"

I blinked at him in confusion. "Why what?"

"I'm a little unclear as to why you showed up on the scene. Did you have some reason to think that Mr. Millard—?"

"Aaron called me. He was on his way to talk to me when he was run down. He said he had something to tell me. Something I needed to know. Just in case."

"Sounds like you and he were friends. I'm sorry for your loss."

"Don't you get it? I don't think this was an accident. I think whoever hit him did it on purpose." My accusation earned a scowl that deepened when I added, "It was probably the same person who broke into his house."

Fleming's eyes, a shade darker than his brows, narrowed. "What's this about a break-in?"

"He *must* have reported it. It happened sometime last week."

"Waycross Springs PD is a small department. I'd have heard about it if he had."

"He told *me*. I was out of town at the time, but we talked about it when I got back."

Although Aaron had made his opinion of the local police crystal clear at the time, I'd still assumed he'd tried to report the crime. That's what I would have done.

"Why don't you fill me in now," Officer Fleming suggested.

The story took a while to tell. I'm not usually given to weeping, but I had to keep stopping to dab at my damp eyes and clear my throat.

"Was anything stolen?" Fleming asked when I'd explained why we'd been having our celebratory lunch, described the bruises I'd seen, and repeated everything Aaron had said about his intruder.

"No."

"Then that probably explains why Millard didn't contact us."

"But—"

He cut me off by surging to his feet. When he held out a hand to help me up, I ignored it, rising easily on my own before taking a step away from him. If he didn't understand the significance of what I'd told him, I'd have to talk to someone else who could—the chief of police, or maybe a deputy with the county sheriff's department.

Aaron's body had been taken away while I'd been sitting on the grass. The crowd of gawkers had dispersed. Only a couple of men in uniform remained and one of them was headed for his patrol car.

"I'll give you a lift back to your shop," Fleming said.

"I can walk."

"Forgive me for saying so, but you look a little wobbly." When I opened my mouth to object, he grinned. "Don't make me arrest you."

Startled, I sent him a hard look. There was a rather attractive glimmer of amusement in his dark eyes, but I had a feeling it was at my expense. "Is that cop humor?"

His sigh was audible. "Look, Ms. Veilleux, you've had a shock. A friend of yours just died under tragic circumstances. I don't want you keeling over on your way back to Main Street. Get in the damn cruiser."

"Well, when you put it so nicely . . ."

I caught myself just before I could smile at him. What was *wrong* with me, all but flirting with this clod of a policeman? He was right, drat him. I was still reeling from seeing what had happened to Aaron.

I got into the police car without further protest and even remembered to thank Officer Fleming when he dropped me off at the studio, but I was no less troubled by my memory of Aaron's last words to me. He had been killed by a hit-and-run driver on his way to tell me something important. If he hadn't been walking along that stretch of road, in the breakdown lane because there were no sidewalks in that part of town, he might still be alive.

Was it guilt making me want to blame his death on a deliberate act of violence? I knew I wasn't responsible for what had happened to him. Not exactly. But I did feel an obligation to try to find out why he'd been so determined to talk to me. Whether his death had been accidental or not, I needed to discover exactly what it was he'd wanted to say.

THE NEXT MORNING I took a break from clearing out the studio to simply walk around Waycross Springs. I'd already concluded that it was a pretty

New England village that reminded me a bit of the town I lived in until I was seventeen. As it had been *before* its growth spurt. Sadly, places changed. Nothing stays the same.

Typical of East Coast villages, the streets in Waycross Springs meandered. Forget being laid out on a grid. Walking in a generally easterly direction along Main Street I came to a redbrick fire station and a white clapboard church with a steeple. The aptly named Park Street took me downhill to a small park with a gazebo at its center. As soon as the weather was warm enough to make sitting outside enjoyable, benches had been set up here and there.

At the foot of the hill, I came out onto East Depot Street. Once upon a time, there had probably been a train station nearby, but most railroad tracks in Western Maine had disappeared decades earlier.

The sound of rushing water drew me across the street to where, down an embankment, a stream flowed rapidly over submerged rocks. Off to the right, it wound behind a series of shops. To the left, it cut in front of an imposing stone structure built on a bit of a hill. Intrigued, I walked toward it and discovered it was Waycross Springs Public Library. I had to cross a bridge to reach the entrance and once I'd gone that far, I couldn't resist going inside.

The moment I stepped through the building's heavy oak front door, I could smell two of my favorite scents—old books and new ones. The silver-haired librarian who'd been adding several volumes to the shelf marked RECENT ARRIVALS turned toward me with a friendly smile.

"Hello," she said. "You must be new in town. I'm Lila Jackson, the head librarian. Well, actually the only librarian. Welcome."

"I'm Val." I didn't identify myself further, since I didn't want the first topic of conversation to be Aaron's death. Instead I asked where I might find something on the history of Waycross Springs.

Lila was no more than five-feet-three, her lack of height made even more obvious by the fact that she'd kicked off her shoes and was walking around in a pair of white crew socks. That alone made me like her.

"You've come to the right place for information." She led me into the library's reading room and waved me toward one of the long tables. "Have a seat."

It was a big open area with a high ceiling and large, gracious windows that looked out over the town. The effect should have been austere and, given the expanse of glass and the fact that it was still April in New England, decidedly chilly. Instead, radiators pumped out heat, dispelling any drafts, and the shelves that filled every available inch of wall space made the room feel downright cozy. I nodded to the room's occupant, a redhead seated in an armchair. Then I simply soaked up the atmosphere until Lila returned with a slim pamphlet in one hand and a heavy, leather-bound tome under the other arm.

Plunking both down on the table at the center of the room, she waved me into a chair and took the one opposite me. "Why don't I give you the capsule version while you look through these?"

"That sounds like a plan. Go for it."

While I turned pages, pausing now and again to study one of the high quality black-and-white photographs used as illustrations, Lila summarized the historical highlights. Waycross Springs had been founded in the early nineteenth century and had been moderately famous for manufacturing shoes until the mid-twentieth. The Sinclair House, a late nineteenth century luxury hotel that was still in business, had once brought even greater prosperity to the town by bottling the water from the spring on its grounds. That business had eventually become unprofitable and been abandoned and, as I'd already surmised, both passenger and freight rail service had been phased out long ago.

"On the bright side," Lila concluded, "there's now a movie theater in the old railroad depot and the shoe factory has been converted into offices and a restaurant."

"So the economy is good?"

Lila waggled her hand in a "so-so" motion. "I won't lie to you. Times are hard in rural areas like this one, but we're doing better than a lot of places. We have shops that appeal to tourists. With several major ski areas less than an hour's drive from here, we draw in a fair number of those folks. And, of course, in the fall we get scads of leaf-peepers who come to gawk at the foliage."

"Spoken like a proud descendant of an old Waycross Springs family."

Lila chuckled. "To tell you the truth, I've only lived here for a couple of years. I'm barely considered a permanent resident and I'll never be a true Mainer." She bowed her head as if ashamed, although her eyes sparkled with self-deprecating humor. "I was born in Rhode Island," she confessed in a hushed whisper.

It was impossible not to like the sprightly librarian. After knowing her for less than an hour, I felt comfortable asking her why she'd chosen to relocate to such a small place.

"I came to spend a little time with my sister and never left. She moved to Waycross Springs some thirty years back, so she's not considered a native, either, but her husband, *he* was born here, so the locals are reasonably tolerant of us both."

I was uncertain how seriously I was meant to take that remark. "How do the locals react to someone settling here who has no connection to the area?"

"Well, that, my dear, depends entirely on the individual. If you're talking about yourself, I'd say you'll have no trouble making friends. Most people here are very welcoming, especially to a newcomer who is outgoing and shows an interest in the community. On the other hand, if a stranger holds back and keeps to himself, everyone tends to leave him alone. It's not that they're unfriendly, just respectful of another person's privacy."

"That wouldn't work very well for someone who is shy."

"True enough, but I don't imagine shyness has ever been a problem for you."

"Just the opposite," I admitted. "Some people find me too pushy, and good old-fashioned curiosity sometimes makes me poke my nose in where it isn't wanted."

A library patron arrived just then. Lila rose to check in the books he was returning and help him find a new one he was anxious to read. The redhead in the armchair looked up from her book and sent me a tentative smile. "You bought Aaron Millard's studio, didn't you? It was such a shame when Aaron shut his doors. I used to have him do copy work for me. Old family photos I wanted to preserve. Of course, that was before scanners got so inexpensive. Still, I used to stop in now and again, just to chat with him. He was an interesting guy." She looked curiously at the camera around my neck. "Do you plan to reopen the studio?"

"I do. I'm Val."

"Annie Denton. I'm the local vet. Small animals, mostly cats and dogs, although I do treat the occasional horse."

Without thinking, I grinned and said, "We have something in common then. A lot of my income derives from shooting pets."

The appalled look on Annie's face had me scrambling to explain myself.

"With a camera. One of my specialties is photographing cats and dogs. I've done several calendars and a coffee-table book."

Annie blinked at me. "Val? Not Valentine Veilleux?"

Surprise restricted my response to a nod. I'm not used to being recognized.

"I have your book. It was given to me as a Christmas present. The pictures are gorgeous."

"Thank you."

"Are you going to do another?"

"I don't know. Maybe. First I have to get settled. But I'm delighted to have met you. I have a cat. She'll need her annual checkup in a couple of months."

I wanted to ask her more about Aaron, but when several more patrons entered the library, Annie got up to leave, explaining that she had a patient due at her clinic in half an hour.

THREE DAYS LATER I was in my RV, concentrating on the images on the screen in front of me, when someone rapped authoritatively on the door. I swiveled in the chair in front of my custom-built work station, located where most RVs put a U-shaped dinette, and leaned forward to peer through the window behind the sofa. My oversized motor home took up one of the spots reserved for business owners in the town's municipal parking lot. I was certain its presence had aroused curiosity among my new neighbors, but until now no one had paid me a visit.

The man waiting impatiently outside wore the uniform of a Waycross Springs police officer. I took a moment to study what I could see of his features. He was older than the other officers I'd met, perhaps fifty or fifty-five, with a jowly face and deep-set blue eyes. I had an excellent view of the latter when he turned his head to stare back at me.

"Open up, Ms. Veilleux," he said in a gravelly voice. "I need to talk with you."

My cat, Lucky, who had been sleeping on the sofa, stood up and stretched. She didn't seem alarmed, only curious. Taking that as a good sign, I left my desk chair to unlock the door and invite the officer in.

He sent me a suspicious look before entering the step well. I moved out of his way. Since space was at a premium, I backed into the kitchen area and waved him toward the front of the RV, the only area where there's room to entertain. Three people can sit on the sofa, if they're good friends, and with addition of my desk chair and the driver's and passenger's seats, I can accommodate a maximum of six.

"Would you like the grand tour?" I asked politely when the officer stopped, hands on hips, to study my living space.

"Not much to it." His tone was insultingly dismissive.

I bristled at the implied criticism. This had, after all, been my home for a good many years. My living quarters might be cramped, but they were comfortable. Besides my office with its state-of-the-art computer workstation, where I edited photographs and created my calendars, the RV boasts a galley-style kitchen, a bath that squeezes in a shower stall as well as a sink and a toilet, and a bedroom with a queen-size bed. I lack none of the necessities of modern life. The bedroom has a television and media center and the kitchen boasts a stove, refrigerator, and microwave.

"I don't believe I caught your name," I said, forcing a polite smile onto my face.

His thin lips twisted into a parody of a smile. "Don't believe I threw it. I'm Brent Gilroy, chief of police." He brushed cat hairs off the sofa before dropping heavily onto the center cushion. "Sit yourself down, Ms. Veilleux. Tell me about this alleged break-in at Aaron Millard's house."

I wondered where Lucky had disappeared to, but wasn't overly concerned. From force of habit I kept an eye out for escape attempts every time the door opened. The cat had not gotten out when Chief Gilroy came in.

I resumed my seat in my ergonomically correct swivel chair and tried to relax. I'd been trying to share my concerns about Aaron Millard's death with someone in authority ever since it happened. I'd gotten the runaround every time. When I went to the police station in person, I was turned away by the secretary/dispatcher. A phone call to the county sheriff's department was no more successful. The unspoken message from both entities was the same: "Don't call us; we'll call you."

"I appreciate your taking the trouble to come here." I hoped I didn't sound as sarcastic as I felt. "I gather Aaron Millard never reported the break-in at his house?"

"You gather correctly. When was this crime supposed to have occurred?"

I ignored the fact that he put the word in air quotes and answered as succinctly as I could. "I'm not sure of the date. It was before I returned to town. Aaron probably wouldn't have told me about it at all if I hadn't noticed that he'd been injured."

Gilroy blinked once, slowly. "What kind of injuries?"

"Bruises."

As I indicated the areas where I'd seen black-and-blue patches, I wondered why the chief didn't already know about them. Hadn't Officer Fleming bothered to give his superior any details? Had he included his interview with me in his report at all?

"When I asked Aaron about them," I continued, "he told me someone broke into his house one night while he was asleep. When he got up and confronted the man, the thief knocked him down and ran away."

"Why didn't he report this?"

"If you knew Aaron Millard at all, you can probably guess."

"Stubborn old cuss didn't trust the police to do right by him."

"Exactly. I don't know what he had against your department, but he seemed convinced contacting you wouldn't do any good. He said he didn't recognize the man, and that he didn't know what he was after. He clearly wanted me to drop the subject, so I did, but I couldn't help but think about it after he was killed."

"Why?" Gilroy's skepticism was back in full force.

"He was on his way to talk to me when he was run down. He'd phoned me earlier. He said there was something he needed to tell me about. Something I ought to know, *just in case*."

"Just in case of what?"

"He didn't say, but there was something about the *way* he said those words." I held up both hands in a gesture of confusion. "I can't explain it logically. All I know is that his voice sounded . . . odd."

"Afraid?"

"Worried, at the least. And a bit grumpy, too. Well, you say you knew him. He liked being thought of as a curmudgeonly old coot. It would have gone against the grain to admit to weakness." I frowned, struck by a new thought. "It was almost as if he was worried about *me*. Whatever he wanted to tell me might have been more of a warning, if that makes any sense."

"And you think someone ran him down to keep him from sharing this information, whatever it was?" The chief shook his head as he started to get up. "You think he was going to reveal some big secret that got him killed? I think you've got an overactive imagination, Ms. Veilleux.

I glared at him. "Have you caught the hit-and-run driver?"

"Not yet. We're working on it."

Now that I had a greater understanding of Aaron's opinion of Waycross Springs's police force, I didn't put much faith in his chance of success. "Do you know anything about the car? Do you have any description of it or the driver?"

"I'm not at liberty to share that information." He headed for the door.

"What about the break-in?" I called after him. "Are you going to look into that?"

He turned to glower at me. "What is it you think we'd discover after all this time?"

"Fingerprints?"

He gave a derisive snort. "Look, Ms. Veilleux, you've done your civic duty and reported what you know. Now leave it to us, okay? If Aaron Millard wasn't just spinning a tale to get sympathy from a pretty young woman, then I doubt this attempted burglary where nothing was stolen had anything to do with his unfortunate death. He was just in the wrong place at the wrong time."

It was clear he didn't believe there had *been* a break-in. It seemed equally obvious that this interview could only end one of two ways. He would either issue a stern warning not to waste any more police time, or he would tell me not to worry my pretty little head about anything anymore because the big strong men of the Waycross Springs Police Department would take care of things.

He surprised me by stopping in the step well to turn my way and ask a question I wasn't expecting. "Do you own a car, Ms. Veilleux?"

It took me a moment to stop gaping at him. "Are you asking me if I was the one who ran Aaron down?"

He smirked. "Just covering all the bases."

"I'm a newcomer, so that makes me a suspect?"

He didn't bother to reply. He simply waited for me to answer his question.

"No, I do not own a car. I have this RV and a bicycle." I gave him the standard spiel to explain the life I'd lived on the road. "When I came through Waycross Springs back in February," I said, "I saw the for-sale sign on the studio. I was interested in settling down, so I met with Aaron. Fortunately for me, he decided I was the buyer he'd been waiting for. We didn't know each other very long, but we were *friends*. Why on earth would you think I'd want him dead?"

"Why would anyone want him dead? We'll find the driver, and when we do, we'll throw the book at him, but don't expect the charge to be premediated murder." He started to leave, then once again turned back. "Let me give you a bit of unsolicited advice, Ms. Veilleux. If you want to fit in here in Waycross Springs, don't make waves."

LATER THAT SAME DAY, the phone rang. My caller ID informed me that the law office of Newbury and Newbury was on the other end of the line. I hesitated, very nearly letting the call go to voice mail, but curiosity won out over caution at the last minute.

"Hello?"

"Is this Valentine Veilleux?" someone asked a mellifluous voice.

"Yes, it is. And you are?"

"Wanda Newbury, Ms. Veilleux. I'm a lawyer. I'd like to speak to you in connection with the estate of the late Aaron Millard."

I held the phone away from my ear and stared at it.

"Ms. Veilleux?" Impatience leaked into the lawyer's tone.

"I'm here. I'm just . . . confused. Does this have something to do with his death?"

"In a manner of speaking. He left you a bequest in his will. Are you free to come by my office this afternoon? I'd prefer not to discuss this matter further over the phone."

Still bewildered, I agreed to a meeting in an hour's time.

The offices of Newbury and Newbury turned out to be a one-story clapboard building on a small lot at the corner of Holland and Middle Streets. I reached it after a brisk ten-minute walk from the photography studio and stood staring at the exterior for a long moment before I went inside. There was no receptionist on duty. At the sound of the door opening and closing, a muffled voice issued from the inner room.

"Come on back, Ms. Veilleux. I'll be with you in a moment."

Wanda Newbury was on the phone when I entered, seated behind an enormous, heavily carved oak desk. She motioned for me to take a seat in one of the two surprisingly comfortable visitor's chairs. While I waited, I studied her. She was a big woman with large hands. Her light brown hair was cut so that it feathered around her face, softening a square jaw. Dark brown eyes flicked my way, making her own assessment after she disconnected.

We were about the same age, in our mid-thirties, and when she stood to reach across the cluttered surface of the desk and offer to shake my hand, I saw that she was only a few inches taller than I am.

"You said on the phone that Aaron Millard left me something in his will. I can't imagine why he'd do such a thing. We hadn't known each other very long."

Wanda Newbury resumed her seat. "It's simple enough. Mr. Millard liked you. Shortly after he agreed to sell you his studio, he had me add a codicil to his will. He left you his cameras."

I felt incipient tears prickle at the back of my eyes and blinked to keep them at bay. I couldn't help but feel deeply moved by the gesture. The cameras were the only things he'd taken with him from the studio when he went out of business. I doubted there was anything that had meant more to the old man.

Wanda leaned back in her chair and studied me through narrowed eyes. "I thought you'd be disappointed."

"What? Why?"

"He didn't have any family. Maybe you thought he'd leave you everything."

"He had no reason to. When you get right down to it, we only met a handful of times. Mostly we talked shop."

"I have a feeling you knew him better than most people. He kept himself to himself, as the saying goes."

Once again a wave of sadness swept through me. "If he didn't have any family, what's being done about a funeral?"

"There won't be one. He left instructions that he be cremated and scattered. No fuss. No muss. I took care of that for him yesterday."

Feeling oddly bereft, I stood. There didn't seem to be any point in staying longer. "When can I retrieve the cameras?" I asked. "I assume they're still at his house."

"I can take you now if you like. I've been meaning to go over there and start work on an inventory of the contents. Once you take your inheritance, everything else is to be put up for sale at an estate auction. The proceeds will go to the local food pantry."

A SHORT TIME LATER, Wanda unlocked the door and gestured for me to precede her into the house. After a moment's hesitation, I stepped inside. This was the simplest and most efficient way to collect my inheritance, but it seemed strange to enter Aaron Millard's home without him there.

He hadn't accumulated many possessions in eighty-three years of life. Wanda ushered me into the living room where, just as I remembered, the camera cases were stacked in one corner. The only furnishings were a rather ratty area rug, a Canadian rocker with sun-faded upholstery, and an end table of the sort sold in discount stores.

"Aaron spent most of his time in the kitchen," I said as I crossed to the corner to examine the cameras.

Given the chill in the room, it belatedly dawned on me that the kitchen was probably the warmest place in the house. No wonder both his comfortable recliner and his television were in that room.

"It doesn't appear you'll have much to auction off." I collected my inheritance and turned back to Wanda.

"Sadly true," she said. "The other rooms don't have much in the way of furniture either. I can't say for certain, but it looks as if he'd been selling off his possessions for some time now to raise enough cash to pay his bills and buy food. I hope, at least, that he got a reasonable price for his business when he sold it to you."

I told her how much I'd paid, watching the lawyer's face as I spoke. When Wanda was unable to hide her surprise, my heart sank. "Let me guess. There wasn't anywhere near that much in his bank account, or under his mattress."

"I can't give you that information."

"Did you *check* under the mattress? He insisted on the bank giving him cash."

Wanda's eyes strayed to the ceiling. "Excuse me a moment, would you?"

Not a chance, I thought, and followed her into the hall and up a gently curving staircase to the second floor.

Aaron's bedroom was unheated and contained little more than the bed, a bureau, and a substantial number of blankets. There was no money under the mattress and nothing hidden in any of the drawers. Wanda even took each one out and checked the bottom, just to be sure he hadn't taped something there. The closet yielded a few items of clothing, much worn. I went through the pockets and patted the linings and hems. I felt a little foolish, since I was basing the search on techniques seen in the movies and on television, but there certainly should have been some money left. Surely Aaron hadn't had time to spend it all before he died.

We searched the rest of the upstairs rooms and even ventured into the attic, but had no better luck. The other rooms were unfurnished and the attic was empty save for a heavy coating of dust and cobwebs. Nowhere was there any clue to indicate what Aaron Millard had done with the proceeds from the sale of his photography studio.

Back downstairs again, Wanda checked the dining room and kitchen while I volunteered to take a look in the cellar. The stairs went steeply down from a door in the hall to an exit at the side of the house. The building was set into the side of a hill, so that the basement beneath the front half was aboveground. At the exterior door, the steps took a sharp turn to the left and continued down until they ended at a concrete floor. I reached up to pull on the long string that turned on a dim electric bulb. Although the illumination was not the best, it was enough for me to see that, like the rest of the house, the cellar was nearly empty. A washer and dryer held pride of place next to the furnace Aaron had obviously stopped using some time ago.

I peered into the dim reaches beneath the back of the house and frowned. Half of that wall appeared to be farther away than the rest. Wishing I had one of those high-powered flashlights instead of just the dim light from my cellphone, I went to investigate, walking cautiously even though the surface was level. The string for another bare lightbulb brushed across my face, eliciting a sharply indrawn breath before I realized what it was and gave it a tug.

A small room had been constructed in the back corner of the cellar. It might have been a storage closet, or a spare bathroom, but even before I opened the door I had a strong suspicion about what I would find inside.

Aaron Millard hadn't needed to borrow the darkroom at the studio. He had another one right here at home.

I inspected the setup with professional interest. The equipment was old but perfectly functional. He'd had everything he needed to develop photographs. More interesting still, it looked as if he'd done at least a little darkroom work in the not-too-distant past. Unlike so much of the rest of the house, in this little room there was hardly any dust.

Neither were there any negatives or prints.

"Huh," said a voice from behind me.

I started, then relaxed when I saw it was only Wanda.

"This equipment should be worth something at auction," I said, "although not many people are into doing photography the old-fashioned way anymore."

"Something's off here," Wanda said.

I waited, but when the lawyer said nothing else, I felt compelled to pry. "I know you aren't supposed to reveal a client's confidences, but your client is dead and you're right. Something *is* off. Did you know this house was burgled shortly before Aaron was killed?"

Wanda sent me an incredulous look. "I didn't hear anything about that."

"Neither did the police. Aaron never reported it. He wouldn't have mentioned it to me if I hadn't insisted he tell me how he got such nasty bruises here and here." I indicated their location on my own body.

Wanda sighed. "You'd better tell me all you know about the incident, but let's adjourn to Aaron's kitchen first, where we can both sit down." It was also the only room with more than one chair.

After I told Wanda what I knew about the break-in and Aaron's struggle with the intruder, I added my suspicions about the hit-and-run being deliberate and made a point of telling Wanda about the total uninterest shown by members of the Waycross Springs Police Department.

The lawyer looked thoughtful but made no comment.

"Your turn," I prompted. "There's something strange going on here and if we pool our resources, we may be able to figure out what it is."

"I suppose, since you are one of Aaron's beneficiaries, you have a right to know a few more details from his will. If there had been a formal reading, you'd have been present to hear it."

"That sounds logical to me."

"He named my law firm as executor. That's my father and me. As I've already told you, he left instructions as to the disposition of his remains and instructed us to sell everything and give whatever the sale raises to the local food pantry." She shot me a look. "And if you're thinking someone there murdered him for the money, think again. It's the local church that sponsors it and I haven't yet told the pastor about the will. From the look of things, the food pantry isn't likely to get much out of the deal. Selling what's here will just about cover the costs of Aaron's cremation."

"You can sell the house itself. It must be worth something."

"Can't. Aaron Millard had a reverse mortgage. This belongs to the bank now."

"I wonder why he didn't sell this place outright and live in the apartment above the studio. It's a perfectly nice place. I'm planning to move in there myself."

"I didn't know him well, but he had a reputation for being a stubborn old coot. I assume he held onto this place, just barely, with the income from the reverse mortgage and his social security checks. But that's what I find so peculiar. I haven't come across *any* financial records in my search of the house. No paperwork of any kind. That means I have no explanation for what happened to the proceeds from the sale. Surely he didn't have debts amounting to as much as he got from you."

"I suspect his insistence on waiting for the 'right buyer' rather than letting the studio go to someone who wasn't a photographer made the situation worse. He must have had to keep paying taxes and insurance on it, and if he didn't have much money to spare, that could have been a heavy burden."

"I have no explanation for any of this," Wanda admitted. "I ought to have found a checkbook, bills, receipts. Everyone keeps *some* financial records, if only for tax purposes."

"I'm surprised he didn't sell the cameras. I haven't had a chance to look them over yet, but I suspect they're all top quality. One or two may even be considered collector's items."

"You did well out of the deal then."

"Hey! I'd much rather that Aaron was still around. And I'd definitely like to know what he intended to tell me the day he was killed."

"There is that." Wanda looked around the room, as if she hoped inspiration would strike. "I doubt we'll ever know what was on his mind."

"It's a pity there wasn't a funeral. We might have talked to the people who came and—" I broke off when I saw the look on Wanda's face. "What?"

"If you're thinking you could have gathered potential suspects together, you're living in a dream world. This isn't an episode of *Masterpiece Mystery*. Besides, if there's anything suspicious about Aaron Millard's death, it's up to the police to look into it."

"But there *is* something suspicious. The hit-and-run driver who killed him hasn't been found."

"And may never be. That doesn't mean it was deliberate."

I didn't agree. My thoughts had moved in a different direction. "What about holding a memorial service? You know—a celebration of life."

"I don't think that's a good idea."

"Why not? I'd have to do a bit more cleaning and rearranging first, but it could be held at the photography studio. I still have all the albums of photos Aaron took when he was shooting weddings and the like. It would—"

"Aside from the sheer foolishness of *trying* to flush out an alleged murderer, it's not what he'd have wanted."

I let the subject drop, but I didn't give up on the idea. Maybe the mysteries surrounding Aaron Millard's death would sort themselves out without my help, but if they didn't, what would be the harm in an informal gathering of those who had known the old man? It would be illuminating just to see who showed up. Then I could talk about Aaron to those who did and, with any luck, I'd discover if anyone had any idea what it was he'd wanted me to know "just in case."

IT WAS THAT EVENING before I had a chance to properly examine my new cameras but I already knew I'd inherited treasure. Two of the camera cases were leather. The others were of more modern vintage, but still predated the era of digital cameras. Each of the five carried the logo of a top-of-the-line camera manufacturer: Nikon, Canon, Leica, Pentax, and Hasselblad.

It was my examination of the Nikon that set my heart pounding. There was undeveloped film still inside the camera. It was unlikely to have anything to do with what Aaron had wanted to tell me, but I couldn't help but be intrigued by the possibilities.

Lifting the camera, I aimed it at my favorite subject—Lucky the cat—to use up what remained of the roll. Then I grabbed a flashlight and my keys and left the RV. Within minutes I was standing in Aaron Millard's darkroom.

No, I corrected myself. *It's my darkroom now.*

Although it had been years since I'd developed black-and-white 35-mm film, the process came back to me with no trouble at all. I'd already spent some time in the darkroom making sure all the equipment was in good working order and that the ventilation was adequate—all darkrooms need good ventilation because of the toxic chemicals involved. Wearing gloves and goggles, I'd measured and mixed those in advance. Now, in the requisite total darkness, I opened the film canister, loaded the film onto a reel, and inserted it into the developing tank. As soon as the film was safely in the tank with the developer solution and the top of the tank was securely attached, it was safe to turn on the lights.

Almost done, I thought with satisfaction a short time later. The steps had to be carefully timed, but they were simple enough. The developer had been followed by a stop bath and then by a session with the fixer. I had agitated the tank as required and rinsed repeatedly under running water. Now it was time to use a wetting agent to prevent water marks forming on the film while it dried. After a thirty-second soak in that mixture, I removed the film from the reel and used film clips to hang the wet negatives from a line.

I had to contain my impatience for the next two hours. It would be folly to handle the film before it was completely dry.

When I returned to the darkroom, I held the negatives up to the light, squinting at the small images in an attempt to see what they were. I couldn't tell much. There were people in most of the shots, and they all seemed to have been taken outdoors. Beyond that, I'd have to wait until I'd made prints.

With four trays set up, left to right, one with developer, one with a stop bath, one with fixer, and the last with water as a final wash, I was ready to go. Working with only the illumination from a safelight with a light amber filter, I positioned my negatives in the enlarger and paper in the printing frame. Once I exposed the paper, I slid it into the developer, emulsion side down at the start. Again timing carefully, I turned it over, agitated it, and tipped up first one side and then the other.

When the process was complete, I hung the print up to dry. It was, in fact, not a single photograph but rather a proof sheet containing small images of all the negatives, but now I could see what was in each shot much more clearly. With the overhead light on once more and with the help of a magnifying glass, I was able to identify Aaron's subject.

With growing concern, I moved the glass from picture to picture. I was not mistaken. The focus of *every* picture appeared to be the same person—Lila Jackson, the librarian.

Working steadily, I produced 8x10" prints of all of the photos on the roll. Once they had been hung up to dry, there was no longer any question in my mind. Aaron Millard had been *stalking* Lila.

I had no idea what to do with that information.

I WAS STILL PONDERING the implications of those photographs the next day when my neighbor, bookstore owner Jonah Abrams, invited me to have lunch with him at Aphrodite's. I didn't hesitate to accept. I already knew the food was terrific.

"I have an ulterior motive," Jonah admitted after we placed our orders.

"Oh?" I felt my eyebrows shoot up.

Jonah was a rotund little man, sixty if he was a day and bald as a cue ball. I didn't expect him to hit on me, but I was wary of the possibility he'd taken a look at my unorthodox lifestyle and decided I was fair game.

His bright blue eyes twinkled with amusement. "Relax. I'm only after you to join our local Small Business Association."

Feeling my face warm, I hastily apologized.

"No need. For all you know I could be an ageing roué who goes after anything in a skirt."

"In that case, I don't need to worry. I rarely wear anything but blue jeans."

"Good one. Now let me tell you about the Waycross Springs Small Business Association. It's too bad you weren't here yet in the fall. We have our annual dinner at the Sinclair House in late October or early November every year. It's a great opportunity to network."

Over sandwiches and drinks, Jonah continued to sing the praises of the organization. He told me a little about some of the other members, making it sound as if every other shop owner in town already belonged to the WSSBA.

I waited until he'd polished off a piece of apple pie for dessert before I broached the subject I couldn't seem to stop thinking about. "What do most people in town think, Jonah? Was Aaron Millard just in the wrong place at the wrong time when he was hit by that car?"

His brow furrowed. "What else would they think?"

"I don't know. It's just that . . . well, Aaron was on his way to talk with me that day. He said he had something important to tell me. Something I needed to know. That *accident* prevented him from revealing what that something was."

Jonah started to smile, realized I was serious, and frowned. "What do the cops think?"

"That it was an accident," I admitted. "But Aaron's house was broken into a few days before he died. I just can't help but wonder if there's a connection."

"Huh."

"I know it seems odd to ask, but did Aaron have any enemies?"

Jonah's expression was dead serious, his eyes devoid of any twinkle. "Aaron Millard was a crotchety old cuss. He feuded on and off with a lot of folks. I had a few heated words with him on occasion myself." He polished off the last of the coffee in his mug.

"What did you quarrel about?"

"Leaving trash cans in the alley between our shops." The top of Jonah's head went pink. "I wasn't so good sometimes about taking mine back in after the garbage truck came by."

"We have a garbage service?" This was news to me.

"Not anymore. The guy went out of business so we're back to hauling our own trash to the dump. I mean landfill."

"I think you mean transfer station."

He chuckled. "Hard to keep up with all these politically correct terms. Anyway, Aaron had a few choice words to say about me leaving those cans out. He used to get all het up over the damnedest things. I hate to speak ill of the dead, but he could be an ornery old so-and-so. You know how it is with elderly folks. They don't hold back when it comes to offering opinions and they don't much care if someone gets offended by what they say. People were a little wary of Aaron's temper."

"I liked him," I said, "and he liked me enough to leave me his cameras. They were important to him. It means a lot that he'd pass them on to me."

"Nice gesture," Jonah agreed.

Remembering the film I'd developed, I asked, "How did Aaron get along with the librarian?"

"Lila Jackson? Fine as far as I know. Tell you the truth, I'd be surprised if he'd even met her. She hasn't been here all that long."

If a couple of years wasn't all that long, I wondered how many decades it would be before I was accepted by the community. I didn't ask. Instead, I said, "He must have known her. Every time I visited his place, there was a stack of library books by his chair. Always different ones, too. He must have been a voracious reader."

"Huh. Never knew that about him. In all the time he was in business right next door to me, he never came into my shop to buy a book. I figured he didn't read, except for maybe newspapers and magazines."

He couldn't afford to buy books, I thought. *That's why he borrowed them.*

It struck me as odd that the two men, given their common love of reading, hadn't been closer. That made me wonder if their falling out over the trash cans had been a symptom of some deeper animosity. Unable to think of a way to question Jonah further without offending him, I opted to broach a related matter.

"I've been thinking," I said slowly, "that I might host a memorial service. I could hold it in the photography studio before I reopen. It would be a celebration of his life and work."

"That's a nice idea," Jonah sounded polite but unenthusiastic.

"Do you think anyone would come?"

"Will there be free food?" At my tentative nod, he grinned. "That, and curiosity will bring them in droves. Hey, Henny!"

Henny Horton didn't look up from rearranging the display case at the front of the restaurant. She was adding delectable-looking strawberry tarts to the mouth-watering selection of cupcakes, brownies, and apple turnovers. "There's no need to bellow at me, Jonah."

"Val here is going to throw a party in memory of Aaron Millard."

She did glance our way then, her brow furrowing. "Yeah? Why?"

"Because he didn't have a funeral." It was as good an excuse as any. I wasn't about to reveal my real reason for wanting to meet more people Aaron had known.

"When?"

"I haven't set a date yet."

Henny sent me a suspicious look. "Why put yourself out? You barely knew the old fart."

"That may be so, but I liked him, and he was on his way to visit me when he was struck by that car."

"So this is about guilt?"

I felt myself flush. "Not exactly, but—"

"You didn't kill him."

"Of course not, but—"

"It's a lot of damn foolishness to carry on about someone after they're dead. *They* sure don't care."

"But those who are left behind often find comfort in—"

Henny's snort cut me off. "What? Getting together, stuffing their faces, and telling a lot of damn lies about the dear departed? That's all a funeral amounts to, and where this 'celebration of life' crap came from, I'll never know. When I kick the bucket, just bury me and be done with it." She narrowed my eyes at me. "Seems to me Aaron Millard felt the same way."

Jonah hid a smile behind his hand. "Don't mind her, Val," he said when Henny had gone back into the kitchen. "You go ahead and make your plans and let me know when to be there. I'll make sure every single member of the WSSBA shows up to lift a glass to old Aaron. We'll send him off in style."

I HAD PLENTY TO DO without spending time worrying about who might have had it in for Aaron Millard, but as I cleaned and sorted, made frequent trips to the local transfer station, and considered what furnishings I'd have to buy, my mind kept coming back to the mysteries surrounding his death. Even if the hit-and-run had been an accident, as the police seemed convinced it was, I still had questions. What was it Aaron had wanted to tell me? It had been something important. I felt certain of that.

Two days after my lunch with Jonah, I lay awake, going over everything I knew about Aaron for the hundredth time. Accustomed as I was to shutting out traffic noise and the conversations of my neighbors in adjacent campsites when I was on the road, it took me some time to realize that the faint sounds I'd been hearing weren't normal.

I sat bolt upright in my queen-sized bed and swiveled my head toward the open window that faced the minuscule back porch attached to the photography studio. I'd parked the RV only a few feet from the building. Either the bulb in the lantern-shaped fixture next to the door had burned out, or someone had shut it off using the switch inside Aaron Millard's old office. I cocked my head, listening hard.

I didn't have to wait long before I heard something heavy scrape across the wooden floor on the other side of the back door. The pad of footfalls came next, and then a muffled curse, as if the prowler had stumbled over something in the darkness.

Grabbing my glasses with one hand and my cellphone with the other, I rolled out of bed. I didn't need to turn on the bedside lamp to call 911. As a seasoned solo traveler, I'd long ago programmed it as my number one shortcut. A dispatcher answered on the second ring.

The eyeglasses now firmly in place on the bridge of my nose, I rattled off the pertinent details while I struggled one-handed into my robe and slid my feet into the sturdy moccasins I use as bedroom slippers. I had no idea where the dispatch center was located, but the woman on the other end of the line assured me that she was already in contact with the police in Waycross Springs.

"Help is on the way, dear," she said. "Don't you worry. You just stay where you are and stay on the line."

I might have complied if I hadn't heard a tremendous crash from inside the studio. I stuck the phone into one of the deep pockets in my robe and headed for the back porch, pausing only long enough on my way out of the RV to grab my keys and shut the door behind me so Lucky wouldn't escape.

Cautiously, I unlocked the office door and stepped inside. I paused to listen and heard the faint shuffle of a shoe on a floorboard. The sound came from above my head.

My heart in my throat, I contemplated the stairs. There was no other way out of the apartment over the studio.

Wishing I'd had sense enough to bring a flashlight, I slipped into the middle room. I expected it to be pitch dark in there, but the door opposite stood open. A streetlight shone through the studio's large front windows, recently washed free of years of grime, providing enough illumination for me to avoid most of the obstacles in my path. I stubbed my toe twice. When my knee connected sharply with an out-of-place settee, I couldn't contain a gasp of pain.

I froze, once again listening for sounds from above. I heard nothing, but I pictured the intruder doing the same thing I was.

It had been utter foolishness to enter the building on my own. If I hadn't come to that conclusion independently, the faint sound of a voice coming from my pocket would have driven the point home. I fished for the cellphone and held it to my ear. I didn't dare speak.

"Did you hear me, ma'am?" the dispatcher asked. "An officer from the Waycross Springs Police Department should be pulling up in front of your store right about now."

I bolted out of the middle room and into the front, heedless of what new obstacles might leap into my path. If I bumped into anything, it didn't register. It was only the crunch of broken glass underfoot that slowed me down. The front door was already open. The intruder had gained entry by breaking one of the panels and reaching inside to release the deadbolt.

I stepped outside just as Officer Fleming pulled up to the curb in his cruiser. He was out of the driver's seat the next instant and headed my way.

"Go around back!" I shouted. "He'll try to escape through the door to the parking lot!"

Fleming went.

My momentum carried me onto the sidewalk in front of the building. I stood there, swaying slightly, my breath soughing in and out and my heart pounding as I watched Fleming disappear from view down the alley between the studio and the bookstore. In my last glimpse of him, his hand was moving toward his holster.

I was so intent on watching the narrow passageway, half expecting to hear gunshots at any moment, that I was caught completely off guard when a dark-clad figure rushed out of my front door and knocked me to the ground. It happened so quickly that I couldn't tell if I'd been sideswiped by a man or a woman. I had only enough time to notice that a ski mask concealed the intruder's features.

I lifted myself partway up, trying to get a better look at the fleeing figure, but it was no use. The guy . . . or gal . . . had already disappeared. I still hadn't managed to get my feet under me by the time Officer Fleming emerged from the shadows.

"Are you okay?" he asked.

"I'll live."

My knee stung and was probably bleeding, but I didn't know if that was from running into the furniture or because I'd skinned it when I landed on the strip of lawn between the shop and the sidewalk. Rocks grew better in that tiny plot than grass did.

"I lost him, Did you see which way he went?"

"Toward Aphrodite's. He must have ducked down the passageway between the buildings."

"Damn. He's long gone by now."

Fleming reached down to take my arm just as I propelled myself the rest of the way upward. We'd have ended up in an awkward clinch if the top of my head hadn't slammed into the underside of his jaw. We both jumped back.

"Ow." I reached up to feel for a lump.

"Ya think?" A rueful look on his face, he rubbed his chin, but the concern I saw in his eyes made me think he was more worried about me than himself.

It must have been a trick of the streetlight, I decided a moment later. There was nothing sympathetic in his voice when he began to lecture me on the foolishness of going into the building instead of waiting for him to arrive.

"My building. My responsibility," I shot back, interrupting him in mid-spate.

"God save me from pigheaded women. Did you get a good look at him?"

I shook my head. "I only caught a glimpse. All in black. Ski mask. I can't even be certain he *was* a he."

"Build?"

"Heavier than I am. Probably taller, but that's only a guess. Not noticeably thin or fat."

"In other words, average build and height and no distinguishing features."

"That's about the size of it."

"Was he carrying anything when he ran into you?"

"I don't think so."

"All right. Let's take a look inside."

I followed him in, sucking in a steadying breath before I flicked the switch to turn on the lights in the front room. "Oh, my."

It looked as if a tornado had passed through. Furniture was upended. The scrapbooks Aaron had kept so meticulously had been flung into a corner.

Fleming closed and locked the front door, careful to avoid the broken glass. "I don't want anyone else coming in just yet."

"I'm not worried about nosy neighbors. They'll hear what happened soon enough."

Frankly, I'd be glad of their support. The devastation was even worse in the middle room. Several of the lightweight backdrops used for studio portraits were damaged beyond repair.

"Someone took a knife to these," Fleming observed. "I wonder why?"

"Maybe he was upset because he couldn't find anything worth stealing." I righted one of the light stands, taking what comfort I could from the fact that the bulb hadn't shattered.

"He was searching for *something*."

I turned to stare at him, but he'd already moved on into the darkroom. I followed, finding similar disarray in there. At least nothing had been smashed.

The office had been ransacked as well. One of the drawers in the filing cabinet had been pulled completely out and dropped onto the floor. That must have been the crash I'd heard.

Upstairs, the doors to every closet and built-in cabinet stood open, but there was little else to show that someone had been there. There had been nothing to steal or destroy, since I'd already emptied out the apartment in preparation for a major furniture-buying spree.

"He was up here when I came in through the back," I said. "I could hear him moving around. He must have left searching the second floor until last."

In silence we descended the stairs and went back into the middle room.

"Can you tell if anything is missing? Fleming asked.

"I won't know until I get this mess cleaned up, but I don't think so."

He sent me a hard look. "Do you have any idea what he was looking for?"

"I don't have a clue, but it does seem like a pretty big coincidence that someone broke into both Aaron's house and Aaron's old studio."

"Not that again."

"Yes, that again."

"Okay, say there *is* a connection." He was clearly humoring me. "What would anyone hope to find in here that he didn't get at Millard's place?"

I felt my eyes widen as the answer smacked me upside the head. "His cameras. Aaron left me his cameras."

"Did the thief get them?"

"They weren't here," I called over my shoulder. I was already in the office and heading for the back door.

Fleming caught my arm just before I got outside. "Hold on a minute. He could be in your RV."

I broke free and turned to glare at him. "He's already had plenty of time to find the cameras and take off again."

That wasn't what worried me most. Lucky was also in the RV.

"I go in first." Fleming pushed past me. "There's no sense in taking chances."

He slipped silently into the parking lot and cautiously approached the door of the RV. I breathed a sigh of relief when I saw that it was still closed.

Fleming opened it and advanced into the step well. From that vantage point he could see into almost every nook and cranny, especially after he used the hand that had been hovering over his gun to take a powerful flashlight from his utility belt and use it to illuminate the interior.

When I came up behind him, I saw that nothing had been disturbed. As soon as Fleming moved out of my way, I called softly to Lucky.

"Lucky?" Fleming asked.

"My cat."

"Are the cameras still here?"

I stooped to peer beneath my workstation, the only place I'd had room to store so many camera cases. They were still stacked exactly as I'd left them. I reached into the space, but not to remove them. I aimed for the two bright golden eyes winking up at me and hauled out a small gray bundle of fur.

"THE CAMERAS ARE RIGHT where I left them," I said as I rose with the cat in my arms. "This is Lucky, by the way."

We stood face-to-face in the narrow space between the workstation and the sofa. Fleming did a classic double-take when he got his first good look at my pet. Then he eyed the stump of Lucky's missing leg.

"I'd have called him Lefty myself."

"Her."

I tried to sound offended when I corrected him, but in all honesty I had to admit the name was appropriate. For some inexplicable reason, it also made me want to laugh. With an effort, I erased every trace of amusement from my voice.

"She was crippled for life by a car."

"Yours?"

"No!" Aghast, I gaped at him. "I don't know who hit her. I rescued her."

"I'm surprised you didn't insist the police hunt down the culprit."

That remark earned him a scowl. I hugged Lucky tighter and resolved not to let Fleming bait me.

"Can you tell if anything in here has been disturbed?" he asked.

I looked past him into the kitchen area. I could see straight through to the accordion door that separated my bedroom from the rest of the RV. It stood open, as I'd left it, revealing the tumbled bed covers. I hid my face in Lucky's soft fur, suddenly much too aware that I was wearing only a nightgown and robe.

I cleared my throat. "As you can see, there's no place for anyone to hide and little that an intruder could search without making a mess. I don't think anyone came into the RV. You must have scared him off."

Fleming sat down on the sofa and took a small, spiral-bound notebook out of his shirt pocket. "What's so special about Aaron Millard's cameras? Why did you jump to the conclusion that they're what the would-be thief was after?"

I sank into my desk chair, still holding Lucky in front of me like a shield, and swiveled to face him. "I can't think what else he'd be looking for, especially if he's the same one who broke into Aaron's house."

"*That* again." This time he sounded more amused than exasperated.

"Yes, *that* again. You can't deny that someone broke into the photography studio. He was clearly searching for *something*."

"Point taken. Are these cameras valuable?"

I released Lucky and reached beneath the workstation to haul out my inheritance. "Yes, they are, which has been puzzling me. Aaron was apparently strapped for cash. He could have sold one or more of his cameras to a collector. This one alone would have kept him in food for months."

I handled the case containing the Hasselblad with reverence. "Back when it was new, it probably cost more than a good used pickup truck."

Fleming opened the case with appropriate care, removing the camera and handing it back to me so that he could examine the interior. "Who knew you had these?"

"Aaron's lawyer, Wanda Newbury."

"Anyone else?"

"I mentioned the bequest when I was having lunch with Jonah Abrams in Aphrodite's a couple of days ago."

"Do you remember who else was there at the time?"

I considered, then shook my head. "Other than Henny Horton and Zillah, the waitress, no."

"It probably doesn't matter. A couple of days is more than enough time for everything you said to have been repeated all over town."

"Did *you* hear about the cameras?"

"No, but I did hear about your plan to host a celebration of life." He returned the first case and reached for the second one.

"There was nothing in any of these except cameras," I said, fudging the truth a bit. "I looked when I first brought them home. I didn't find a single cryptic warning or hidden clue."

I did not mention the film I'd developed. There was no way Lila Jackson had been the person who'd broken in.

Fleming sent me a repressive look. "I'm just covering all the bases." He glanced around. "Don't RVs usually have a dinette? It would be easier to examine the cameras if I had a table to put them on."

"Sorry. I had the dinette taken out to make room for my workstation, but if you reach into the space between the sofa and the step well you'll find a folding tray table."

One by one, Fleming dutifully examined each camera and its case, handing them back to me to put away when he was done. When I'd restored the Pentax MX to its case and all five cases to their nest beneath the workstation, I looked a him expectantly.

"What happens now?"

"You make a complaint. I file a report. Since nothing appears to have been stolen, the charges will be breaking and entering and vandalism. Chances of catching the guilty party are slim."

"Can't you take fingerprints or something?"

He sighed. "I'll dust your front and back doors, but anyone who watches TV these days knows enough to wear gloves when committing a crime. And I'll have to take your prints for elimination purposes. Has anyone else had a legitimate reason to touch either door handle recently?"

I began to see the problem. I'd had plumbers and electricians in to update the building's plumbing and wiring and several of my new neighbors had stopped by while I was working on cleaning up the work area and emptying out the apartment.

It was even possible that the intruder *was* one of my neighbors.

"Never mind."

"No. I'll do that much. Just don't get your hopes up."

I glanced through the window behind his head. I had a clear view of the back of my building. Now it was my turn to sigh.

"I'll have my work cut out for me cleaning up the mess he left, and just when I had everything nearly ready for company, too."

"The memorial you've got planned for Aaron Millard? Why are you so set on doing that anyway?"

I shrugged. "Someone should do something to mark his passing, don't you think? I didn't like the feeling that he'd already been forgotten. He lived here all his life. He might not have been the friendliest guy around, but he was part of this community. I want to acknowledge and celebrate that fact."

He regarded me with an enigmatic expression. "You barely knew him."

"I wish I'd known him better. I'm hoping to learn more at his celebration of life, when people have the opportunity to reminisce about him."

"Uh-huh. Are you sure this has nothing to do with proving your theory that someone deliberately ran him down?"

Tired of defending myself, I answered his question with one of my own. "Are the police any closer to identifying the car that hit him?"

Fleming heaved himself upright, towering over me and depriving me of the space necessary to rise from my chair. "A word of advice, Ms. Veilleux."

"Yes?" I infused that single syllable with every ounce of defiance I could muster and saw that he got the message.

He braced his hands on the arms of my chair and leaned in until his face was only inches from mine. "You need to butt out of police business, *especially* if you're still convinced that hit-and-run was deliberate. Any *sensible* person, believing that, would think twice about trying to gather potential suspects together in order to question them. That ploy may work in detective fiction, but it's a recipe for disaster in real life. If you're wrong, you'll embarrass yourself and if, by some fluke, it turns out that you're right, you'll have made yourself a target. I'd hate to see anything happen to you."

"Is that a threat?"

For a brief moment, he looked startled. He released the arms of my chair and straightened. "Not from me, it isn't. It's a warning not to take foolish risks."

Without another word, he turned and left the RV.

WHEN THE DOOR CLOSED behind him, I bounded to my feet and leaned into the step well to engage the lock. Officer Fleming's patronizing attitude left me fuming. Instead of deterring me, his warning made me want to dig in my heels.

I'd been putting off setting a date for the celebration of life, a little daunted by Jonah's promise that the entire membership of the Waycross Springs Small Business Association would attend. *No more procrastinating,* I told myself.

As soon as soon it was late enough for the shops in town to be open, I started making phone calls to let everyone know that Aaron Millard's celebration of life would be held the next evening. After I arranged for the broken window in the door to be replaced, I got to work cleaning up the mess in the studio.

Once I'd cleared the middle room of furniture, props, and light stands to make room, I set up several card tables and a few dozen folding chairs I'd borrowed from the local fire house. Jonah had loaned me two large plastic punchbowls, the ones he used when he hosted book signings. I made the punch myself and bought pastries from Henny. I waffled over the purchase of disposable cups, plates, and cutlery, but even with the prospect of moving from the RV into the apartment, it seemed extravagant to invest in more glassware, dishes, and silverware than I'd need for my own use.

The front room of the studio was next. I soon had the furniture righted and every surface polished to a high gloss. To my relief, the thick albums full of samples of Aaron's work had not been damaged when the intruder flung them onto the floor. Once again, they were proudly displayed on a low table flanked by chairs. Anyone who was interested could sit and go through them to admire the photographs he'd taken.

As six o'clock on the evening of the celebration of life approached, I grew increasingly nervous. What if no one came? What if everyone in town did? I had yet to meet most of the townspeople who would be my neighbors for years to come. I was anxious to make a good first impression, but that didn't mean I wouldn't take advantage of any opportunity that presented itself to question those who attended. There were mysteries surrounding Aaron's life and death. The police might not care about solving them, but I did.

Jonah was the first to arrive. He was closely followed by a striking couple in their mid-fifties who introduced themselves as owners of the Sinclair House, that venerable old hotel on the outskirts of the village.

"You put us all to shame," Mrs. Sinclair said. "No one else gave a thought to honoring Aaron."

"Did you know him well?" I asked.

"I don't think anyone did, but he was a fixture in town for decades. It's good to have a chance to pay our respects."

Their approval of the celebration of life eased some of my nervousness and I turned to greet the next arrivals with considerably more confidence. They came through the door in a steady stream. Ordinarily, I'm good at keeping names and faces straight, but meeting so many strangers all at once made them blur. I was relieved when I spotted Lila.

"I expect you to become a regular patron at the library now that you're settling in here," Lila said after we exchanged greetings.

"I've been meaning to stop by again." I wanted to show her the photographs I'd found in Aaron's camera, but this wasn't the time to mention them.

"No need to apologize. I expect you've been busy." Lila turned to the woman behind her and introduced her as her sister.

I smiled and nodded and tried to steer the conversation toward memories of Aaron Millard.

"He was an excellent photographer," Lila said before she was displaced by new arrivals.

They turned out to be the town's elected officials. The three men looked enough alike to be triplets. I never did get their names straight. It was the woman with them who was the town manager of Waycross Springs.

"It's a wonderful thing you're doing here," she said while she still had my hand grasped in a firm grip.

Her party moved on. Wanda Newbury came in, closely followed by Annie Denton, the veterinarian. By the time I had a chance to look around for Lila again, she and her sister were surrounded by a group of their acquaintances.

In the course of the next hour, several dozen more townspeople put in an appearance. Conspicuous by their absence were any members of the Waycross Springs Police Department. I had expected the chief to show up, and probably Officer Fleming, too.

No one who did come to what some referred to as Aaron Millard's "wake" stayed very long and only a few shared their memories. No one seemed to have known the photographer well. It was left to me to reminisce about the old man's love of jigsaw puzzles, fantasy novels, and TV game shows.

Two hours after I opened my doors, everyone but Jonah and Henny had left. The refreshments had dwindled down to crumbs and a trace of liquid in each of the punch bowls.

"I was really hoping people would share more anecdotes," I confided to my two remaining guests.

"What did you expect?" Henny sounded cranky. "Aaron Millard was a loner. Kept to himself. Loved his cameras more than he did people. What happened to those cameras, anyway? Did you buy them along with the building?"

"Aaron kept them."

I gave Henny a curious look, wondering why she'd asked. She was tall, and broad-shouldered for a woman. For one fleeting moment I envisioned her as my masked intruder. Instead of disappearing down the passageway between the studio and the restaurant, she could easily have ducked into her own building to hide from the police.

I dismissed the notion in the next instant. She was in her seventies, for goodness sake!

Since I had failed to answer Henny's question fully, Jonah filled in the missing part of the answer. "Aaron left Val the cameras in his will."

"Interesting," Henny said as she headed for the door. "I had no idea you and Aaron were so close. Just goes to show you that you never know all there is to know about your neighbors."

THERE WERE AT LEAST two dozen children at the library when I got there the next day. Lila sat on the floor in the room where she and I had talked on my first visit. The long table had been shoved back against the walls to make room for the circle of rapt young listeners who surrounded her. The only person who looked up when I came in was a tired-looking middle-aged woman who sat slumped in the armchair.

I backed rapidly out into the library's main room and headed for the circulation desk. It was manned by a pimply youth with uncombed hair and a nose ring. The faded T-shirt he wore was a souvenir of a long-ago Phish concert.

"Is Ms. Jackson likely to be busy much longer?" I asked.

"Dunno."

He didn't look up from the computer screen in front of him. I had to wonder if he was working on library files or surfing the web.

"How long do these sessions usually run?" I'd heard the term "story hour," but had no idea if that was an accurate description.

This time he spared me a glance and an indifferent shrug. He either didn't know or didn't care and looked bored in the way only a teenager can.

"Let's try this another way. How much longer until the librarian takes over here and you get to leave?"

At that thought, he brightened visibly. He glanced at the analog clock on the wall behind the desk and took a moment to calculate before he answered. "Half hour," he said, and went back to staring at the monitor.

I browsed in the mystery section while I waited and soon lost myself in the sheer physical pleasure of handling volume after volume. I lifted a novel to my nose, sniffed, and smiled to myself. I'd almost forgotten how much I liked that distinctive smell.

Living in the RV, with space at a premium, I'd grown accustomed to doing almost all my reading in electronic format. Now that I was going to be staying in one place, I could borrow books from the local library. Borrow? Heck, I could *buy* them. Once I moved into the apartment, I'd have room to start my own mini-library.

The thunder of little footsteps and the raucous sound of youthful voices all talking at once snapped me out of my reverie. I turned in time to see the harried-looking teacher herd her charges out of the library. Lila emerged, beaming, from the reading room. She looked none the worse for wear, but I didn't suppose she had to deal with rambunctious children more than once a week.

"Hello, Val," Lila greeted me. "I should have warned you last night not to come until after eleven. Mrs. Simon's fourth graders pay regular visits. I'm reading one of Maine author Lea Wait's historical novels to them."

"They seemed to be enjoying it."

"They're good kids and it's a great book." She turned to her young assistant. "Eliot, will you put the room back in order, please? Then you'll be done for the day."

Eliot slouched off in the direction of the reading room. A moment later, I heard the scrape of heavy furniture being shoved across a wooden floor. I winced, but Lila seemed unconcerned.

"Let's get you that library card, shall we?" She slipped behind the circulation desk and clicked a few keys. "Just a couple of questions and you'll be all set."

"I have a couple of questions for you, too," I said.

"I'll bet I know one of them." Lila lowered her voice. "Eliot was assigned here to do community service. He got into a little trouble a few months ago, but he's not really a bad kid." Her lips twitched. "Appearances can be deceiving."

"They certainly can," I agreed.

I spent the next few minutes giving Lila the details she needed to issue a library card. I had to supply both my mailing and street addresses, since they were not the same. Waycross Springs is too small to have door-to-door delivery. One of the first things I did after I moved in was rent a post office box. I also gave Lila the phone number for my cell.

"No landline?"

"I didn't think it was necessary."

"Are you going to have a separate business phone?" Lila asked.

"I hadn't thought about it." I'd used my cell for both personal and business calls when I was on the road. Would things really be that different now?

"Okay. That should do it."

A whirring sound indicated some sort of machine at work beneath the circulation desk. A moment later, Lila handed over a freshly minted library card. It did not have my name on the front, just the name and address of the library. There was a bar code on the back. Clearly, it had been longer than I'd thought since I last checked a book out of a library!

Eliot emerged from the reading room. "All done. Can I go now?"

Lila ignored his surly attitude. "You *may*. I'll see you tomorrow."

"Yeah. Whatever." A moment later he was gone.

I scanned our surroundings. I could see most of the library from where I stood. There did not appear to be anyone else around.

"We need to talk."

"You're very serious. What's wrong?"

"Nothing, I hope. There's no way to ease into this, Lila. I found a roll of film in one of Aaron's cameras and developed it. All the pictures were of you."

Lila frowned. "I don't understand."

"You and Aaron knew each other, right? I mean, I know he used the library. He always had a stack of library books next to his recliner."

"Well, yes. Of course. But I didn't know him outside of the library. He'd closed his studio by the time I moved here. Or maybe shortly thereafter. Now that I think about it, I'm not certain."

"Do you think—?" I broke off, trying to think of a more delicate way to phrase my question. When nothing came to mind, I blurted, "Did he ever ask you out?"

"You've *got* to be kidding!"

"I'm completely serious. Look, I'll show you the pictures." I reached into the tote bag I'd brought with me and pulled out the folder containing the prints I'd made. One by one, I spread them out on the counter.

Lila stared at them, the color leeching out of her face. "How could he have taken these without my knowing? He must have been *following* me."

"That's what it looks like to me," I admitted. "But why would he do that?"

With trembling fingers, Lila swept all the prints together, turned the stack upside down, and shoved it toward me. "I can't believe this."

"Is it possible that Aaron was attracted to you? That he became obsessed?"

"Don't be ridiculous!"

"Then why take these pictures?"

Lila closed her eyes and drew in a deep breath. When she opened them, she reached for the photographs. "Let me see those again."

This time she went through them one by one. When she was done, she looked up and met my worried gaze.

"I'm wearing the same clothes in every one of these. They were all taken on the same day. Sometime last winter by the look of it."

"He never finished shooting the roll of film," I mused. "Never developed it. That makes no sense."

"It makes no sense that he would have stalked me in the first place," Lila said. "We chatted when he came in to exchange library books. That was the extent of our relationship. I never saw any indication that he was interested in me on a personal level."

"Then maybe," I said, thinking aloud, "someone hired him to take those pictures. He was strapped for cash." I shook my head. "That doesn't make any sense either."

A thump jerked my attention back to Lila. The librarian had collapsed into her chair. Eyes wide, she stared at me as if she'd seen a ghost.

"H-h-hired?"

"Lila, what is it? Are you all right?"

"No, I am not all right! This is a nightmare."

Growing more concerned by the minute, I circled the desk and knelt beside Lila's chair. "What is it? Tell me."

Lila glared at me. "Why should I tell you anything? I barely know you. I thought I knew Aaron Millard, and look how wrong I was about that."

Her agitated state alarmed me. She wanted me gone, but leaving was not an option.

"We need to talk. Right now. I'm going to lock the door and put the closed sign up. Just until you get a grip on yourself. Okay?"

I didn't wait for Lila's agreement, but suited action to words. By the time I'd assured our privacy, she was back on her feet and once more flipping through the photographs.

"These show where I work. Where I live."

"Who could have hired Aaron to take them?"

Slowly, Lila resumed her seat, letting the prints fall back onto the counter. "My ex-husband."

I stared at her. "I thought you said you were a widow?"

A grim smile appeared on the librarian's face. "I lied. When I told him I wanted a divorce, he tried to kill me."

"Then why isn't he in jail?"

"A jury acquitted him. After that, I was afraid to stay in the same town. I moved to Waycross Springs because I had family here. I told everyone I was a widow because I wanted to start a new life. I thought I'd seen the last of him, but I can't think who else would have hired Aaron to take those pictures."

I leaned against the desk. Now I was the one who needed the support. "Lila, do you really think your ex is capable of murder?"

"In a New York minute. Especially if he's been drinking." Her eyes narrowed as she took note of my distress. "What are you thinking?"

"This will probably sound crazy."

"Tell me anyway."

"I don't think Aaron's death was an accident. He was on his way to tell me something he said I needed to know. The more I've thought about the way he sounded on the phone that day, the more I think he felt he had to warn me about something . . . or some*one*. What if it was your ex-husband?"

I thought she'd dismiss the idea out of hand, but she surprised me.

"It wouldn't have been that hard for Aaron to find out what happened between me and my husband. Not these days. Do you suppose he did a little research and decided he didn't want to have any part in whatever George had planned for me?"

"That could explain why he never developed the film. And if this George is as violent as you say, and he found out Aaron had double-crossed him, it's possible *he* ran Aaron down."

Lila drew in a deep, shuddering breath and let it out again. "If George knows where I am, why hasn't he come after me?"

"Maybe he meant to, but if he confronted Aaron first and then ran him down to stop him from warning you, maybe he's had to lie low. The police are still looking for the hit-and-run driver. I think we need to tell the local police about these pictures."

"No. No, Val. You're making a mountain out of a molehill."

"Do you want to risk having George show up on your doorstep?"

"If I talk to the police, they'll question him. If he doesn't already know where I am, he'll find out, and then he'll be furious with me for causing him trouble. I can't risk it, Val."

"You can get a restraining order."

"They aren't worth the paper they're printed on. Trust me. I have reason to know that."

We both jumped at the sound of someone knocking. A faint voice called, "I know you're in there. Open up."

"We aren't supposed to close until four today," Lila said. "I need to unlock the door."

I hastily gathered up the photographs and stuffed them back into my tote bag. "Are you going to be okay?"

"I'll manage." She turned just as she reached the entrance. "Promise me you won't say anything about what I've told you to anyone else. We've just been speculating here. There's probably a perfectly innocent explanation for those pictures. We just haven't thought of it yet."

"I'll keep this to myself, for now." I was reluctant to commit to more than that.

THE FOLLOWING DAY DAWNED clear and cool, perfect for the next project on my DIY to-do list. The exterior of my building was in dire need of a fresh coat of paint. Unfortunately, what was already covering those surfaces was badly cracked and flaked. The old needed to be thoroughly scraped off before I could begin to apply the new. Resigned to a boring, backbreaking job, I put down a drop cloth, set up an extension ladder, revved up my iPod and earbuds, and started on the wall that faced Main Street.

The work was going faster than I'd expected when I began to have the uneasy feeling that I was being watched. I'd expected people might stop and stare, but I'd left plenty of room for pedestrians to get around me. I'd carefully positioned the ladder on the foot or so of "lawn" between the sidewalk and the photography studio.

I tried to ignore the sensation, but it didn't go away. That no one spoke made me even more uneasy. When I finished scraping the section of clapboard siding I could reach from where I was and was ready to move down a step, I braced myself mentally, removed the earbuds, and looked for the source of my uneasiness.

The chief of police stood just below and to one side of me. His fists rested on his hips and his lips were flattened into a thin, disapproving line. His belligerently thrust-out chin was level with my knees.

"A word, Ms. Veilleux?" Brent Gilroy said.

Repressing a groan, I descended. When I turned to face him, I drew myself up to my full height, but he still had a few inches on me and was considerably more bulky. That he was also in uniform added to the intimidation factor, but I was determined not to let him see how nervous he made me feel.

"What can I do for you, Chief Gilroy?"

"Are you aware," he asked in a loud voice, his manner aggressive, "that you are in violation of the town's ordinance against littering?"

I blinked rapidly, taken aback by the question. "What on earth are you talking about?"

He pointed to the sidewalk behind my ladder. Not all of the paint I'd scraped off the siding had landed on the drop cloth.

"Oh."

"Oh? Is that all you have to say?"

"I'll clean it up as soon as I finish for the day." I refused to let his blustering turn me into a sniveling coward. "There's really no point in doing it any sooner."

"Don't get smart with me, lady. Are you looking to get arrested?"

"Oh, please." The ridiculousness of the situation overcame my earlier nervousness. Even if my transgression qualified as littering, which I doubted, it was hardly a major crime.

"You'd be well advised to take me seriously."

In my peripheral vision, I saw people stopping to listen. Henny came out of Aphrodite's to see what was going on and Jonah stood in the doorway of the bookstore, watching developments with wary eyes.

I didn't care to be the center of attention and I was beginning to worry that Gilroy wouldn't balk at putting me in handcuffs and stuffing me into the back of the police car parked at the curb in front of the restaurant. Keeping my gaze level and my voice calm, I tried reasoning with him.

"I realize I've inadvertently made a mess, but I *will* clean it up. And surely the other shopkeepers on Main Street would prefer a freshly painted storefront to the run-down façade that's here now. With the job only partway done, it's even more of an eyesore than it was before. If you'll just let me get on with it, I'll be finished in no time."

Gilroy glowered at me. "Do you have a permit for this work?"

The snide tone of his question told my that he wasn't inclined to compromise. It took an effort to speak, what with my teeth gritted and all. "I didn't think I'd need one. This isn't new construction."

"Ignorance of the law is no excuse."

"Leave the girl alone, Brent." Henny's voice was every bit as harsh as the chief's. "She's doing us all a favor fixing the place up like this."

Gilroy swung around to aim his glare in her direction. "Don't know why you're defending her, Henny. The way I hear it, she stole this place right out from under your nose, conning old man Millard into selling it to her instead of to you."

His words momentarily distracted me from my current predicament. I had decided I'd let my imagination run away with me to suspect Henny of breaking and entering, let alone think she was capable of running down a frail old man. Now I wasn't so sure. Had a dispute over the sale of Aaron's building given Henny a motive?

"She's told you she'll clean up the sidewalk when she's done scraping for the day," Jonah interrupted, putting an end to my musings and to any further dialogue between Gilroy and Henny. "Don't worry. We'll all pitch in and make sure the job's done right."

The chief's scowl deepened. "That's as may be, but I'm writing up a citation." He extracted an official-looking pad from the pocket of his uniform jacket. Scribbling rapidly, he began to fill in a form.

Your tax dollars at work, I thought. The man was an imbecile. I was suddenly very glad it had been Officer Fleming who'd responded to my 911 call the other night. I was even happier that I'd agreed not to turn Aaron's photos of Lila over to the local police. Gilroy's priorities were obviously out of whack.

He tore off the top copy and gave it to me. "You can pay the fine at the town office any time you like."

Together with Henny, Jonah, and two strangers who'd been window shopping and stopped to eavesdrop, I watched in silence as he stalked to his cruiser and got in. He slammed the door so hard that it made the window rattle.

After he drove away, I looked at the slip of paper in my hand. My heart sank. Fifty dollars? In the great scheme of things, the fine wasn't all that high, but if it took me several more days to finish scraping the building and I was fined every time a flake of paint landed on the sidewalk or in the municipal parking lot, this DIY project could get expensive fast.

"Give me that." Jonah snatched the citation out of my hand. "I'll speak to the town clerk. She's married to my cousin."

"You don't have to—"

"Consider it a housewarming present," he called over his shoulder as he disappeared into his shop.

Henny and the random spectators had already dispersed. Left with no other practical course of action, I climbed up the ladder and went back to work.

THE NEXT DAY A DELIVERY van pulled up at the curb in front of the photography studio just as I finished applying a coat of primer to the front of the building. I'd ordered all the furniture for my new living quarters online, but it wasn't supposed to arrive until the end of the week. I scrambled down the ladder beset by equal parts of dismay and panic.

At least the rooms were currently empty.

"I wasn't expecting you today," I told the driver when he handed me the bill of lading.

I skimmed the paperwork. There was no mistake. This was my shipment.

"All the furniture goes on the second floor. I guess you can just shove everything inside the apartment and leave it for me to sort out later."

I'd intended to have the delivery men set up each piece in its proper place, but this late in the day they'd be on overtime if they did much more than unload the truck. I directed them to pull the van through the alley into the municipal parking lot.

The sight of my stairwell was enough to earn disgruntled looks from every member of the crew.

"Awful narrow," one said.

Translation: they were going to expect generous tips when they were done.

My new mattress and box springs and just been successfully maneuvered up the stairs and along the equally narrow hallway to my bedroom when Jonah stuck his head in the doorway from the back stoop.

"Looks like you've got your hands full," he observed. "Want me to take care of putting away your painting gear?"

"That would be wonderful."

I didn't have to feign my gratitude. In all the confusion of getting the movers organized, I'd completely forgotten about the ladder, the open can of paint, and the brush and roller in need of cleaning.

About half of my new possessions had been unloaded when I realized that the production had drawn a lot of attention. Several people leaving businesses or offices on their way home from work had paused to gawk at the proceedings before getting into their cars. That didn't surprise me after my earlier experience with the chief of police. Free entertainment is always welcome in a small town.

What did take me aback was seeing Officer Fleming and a man whose name I didn't know walk right into the chaos in my living room and pick up the chest of drawers the movers had just dumped there.

"Which room does this go in?" Fleming asked.

"You don't have to do this," I protested. He wasn't in uniform. I didn't know whether that made his presence harder or easier to accept.

"Neighbors help neighbors around here." He jerked his head toward his companion. "This is Jack Ippolito. Which room?"

I led them back down the hallway and pointed. "That one. Anywhere is fine."

Belatedly, I recognized Ippolito as the first police officer at the scene of the hit-and-run. Even as they placed the chest of drawers against a wall, I heard more footsteps on the stairs. Eliot, Lila's reluctant assistant at the library, appeared. There was no mistaking that nose ring.

"S'posed to help you out," he mumbled.

He looked less than enthusiastic about this alternate form of "community service" but before I could tell him he needn't stay, Fleming caught sight of him.

"Get in here, Carstairs."

Eliot obeyed with the alacrity of a well-trained dog taking orders from his master. The next thing I knew, the three of them had not only assembled my new bed, they'd done a half-decent job of arranging the rest of the bedroom furniture and were starting to work on the kitchen.

Muttering under my breath about gift horses, I concentrated on supervising the movers. In short order, they finished unloading and even put the living room furniture more or less where I wanted it.

Tipping the professionals cleaned out my stash of petty cash. I was contemplating how to repay the volunteers for their help when there was a knock at the apartment door. Without waiting for me to tell her to come in, Zillah entered bearing two of Aphrodite's large pizzas in takeout boxes and a sack bulging with sodas.

"Compliments of Henny Horton." Zillah grinned widely when three hungry males instantly materialized. Jonah, who had returned briefly to his bookshop, wasn't far behind.

We ate in my newly furnished kitchen.

"This was nice of Henny," I said as I dug in.

Jonah snorted. "She's just trying to get on your good side."

"Why, for goodness sake? It's not as if I've been showing her the bad one."

"*Do* you have a bad one?" Jack Ippolito asked, provoking general laughter.

I was surprised by how relaxed I felt in the company of the two police officers. They had a similar effect on Eliot Carstairs. The young man I'd pegged as surly and discontented when I met him at the library had become a different person in their presence. What I'd at first taken for fear of displeasing someone in a position of power now appeared to be a form of adolescent hero worship. Eliot hung on every word Fleming spoke.

"You never know with Henny." Jonah sounded thoughtful.

"What do you mean?" I asked.

"You remember you asked me once if Aaron Millard had any enemies?" At my nod, he continued. "Well, he and Henny didn't always get along, and she's got a hell of a temper."

I drew back in the act of reaching for another slice of pizza. "I still don't see what that has to do with her sending up refreshments."

"I guess I didn't think much about it either, until Henny started being *nice* to you. Pretty strange when you think about it, since she wanted to buy this place and expand Aphrodite's. Aaron refused to sell. He kept saying he was waiting for the right buyer. That'd be you, another photographer. Henny got pretty hot under the collar when she heard the sale was pending. Even told him he'd regret it if he went through with the deal instead of taking her offer."

I was very aware of the silence around my new kitchen table. Eliot had stopped chewing. He looked at each officer in turn, a puzzled and slightly alarmed expression on his face. Jack's gaze was focused on Jonah. Fleming—I still didn't know his first name—was watching me intently.

"What's going on?" Jonah asked.

"Did you know Aaron's house was broken into a few days before he died?" I asked.

"Huh," Jonah said. "Anything taken?"

Eliot suddenly became very interested in his pizza.

Fleming cleared his throat. "If you're thinking that Henny Horton had anything to do with what happened to Millard, you need to get a grip on reality. The woman's seventy-five if she's a day."

"Henny Horton is capable of driving a car, and anyone who cooks all day, every day in a restaurant is no frail blossom."

"Maybe we should let the subject drop," Jack interrupted. "You know how the chief feels about sharing information with civilians."

"Your chief is an obnoxious blowhard," I snapped, "and my concerns about Aaron's death are perfectly legitimate."

Uncomfortably aware that they were all staring at me, and that they were here in the first place because they'd pitched in to help my move into my apartment, I squeezed my eyes shut and counted to ten. "I apologize," I said when I opened them. "I shouldn't have said that."

"Which part?" Fleming asked, sotto voce.

Eliot snickered.

Jack laughed outright.

They had all, apparently, heard about my ticket for littering.

NOTHING MUCH HAPPENED during the following few days. I went to bed completely exhausted, my arms aching from wielding a paintbrush. That I did my sleeping in a comfortable new king-size bed in an apartment completely furnished with brand new, store-bought furniture made me quietly happy. For the first time in a dozen years, I didn't have to drive to a new location every week or two. I reveled in grocery shopping to fill a refrigerator that held more than a two-day supply of perishables, and in cooking on a stove with four burners and an oven big enough to hold a twenty-pound turkey. I even had a out-of-the-way space to stash Lucky's new litter box.

I hadn't splurged, I told myself. I'd made practical choices in decorating my new home. I was holding off on choosing artwork for the walls, rugs for the floors, and knickknacks to display on the built-in shelves. I hadn't yet bought any books. Now that I'd actually moved into the apartment, I could take my time with the details.

For the next little while, I vowed to focus on the final preparations for opening Veilleux's Photography. I'd done a thorough cleaning of all the downstairs rooms after the celebration of life. I'd moved Aaron's photographic equipment back into the darkroom and middle room. His sample books were currently stored in my spare bedroom but I'd kept the low table where they'd been displayed. It was in its accustomed place, along with the chairs he'd grouped around it.

The sales counter in the front room was built in, but a little elbow grease and a generous application of furniture polish had done wonders to restore its appearance. The last item on my to-do list was hanging the framed prints of my photographs and pricing them to sell to tourists.

I was halfway downstairs when the cellphone in my jeans pocket vibrated. Without thinking, I pulled it out and answered.

Near silence greeted me, but if I listened hard, I could hear someone breathing.

I rolled my eyes and disconnected. I don't know which I find more annoying, robocalls or calls from people who've dialed the wrong number. This made the third time in as many days that a caller had stayed on the line without speaking, as if unable to decide what to do next. When *I* misdial, I apologize and then hang up.

An hour later, I'd just positioned the last of the prints when I heard someone rap hesitantly on the glass panel in the front door. I looked down from my perch on top of a stepladder and smiled when I recognized Annie Denton.

"I saw that your lights were on," Annie said when I unlocked the door and opened it. "I took a chance that you wouldn't mind a visitor."

"Perfect timing," I said. "I was just about to take a break."

As Annie stepped past me into the studio, I paused in the doorway to look out across Main Street. A car passed by. A dozen more were parked in front of the line of buildings opposite. A couple came out of the entryway shared by a dentist's office and a computer repair shop. Neither so much as glanced my way, but I couldn't quite shake the eerie feeling that I was being watched. It was a sensation I'd experienced more than once in recent days.

Shaking my head, I'd started to turn away when a flicker of movement between the florist's shop and a store that sold vintage clothing caught my eye. For a moment I froze, staring hard at the rapidly disappearing figure. I wasn't close enough to make out much of his appearance and I hadn't caught even a glimpse of his face, but there had been something familiar about him.

"Val?" Annie asked. "You okay?"

I forced a smile. "I'm fine."

Closing the door firmly behind me, I crossed to where Annie was admiring the photographs displayed on the walls. About half of them were of dogs or cats. The rest were landscapes.

"How about a nice cup of tea? I'd love to show off my newly decorated apartment."

Lucky was waiting for us in the hallway. I grabbed hold of her before she could make a break for freedom and held the little cat cuddled against my chest until the door at the top of the stairs was safely closed again.

"Has she managed to escape yet?" Annie asked.

"Not so far. She won't get past the office even if she does. I worried about her a lot more when we were living in the RV."

"I have heard a door defined as 'that which the cat is on the wrong side of.'" Annie's eyes twinkled as she shared this bit of wisdom.

A short time later we were settled in the living room with tea and cookies, sharing my new sofa while Lucky sat on the window seat industriously washing herself.

"I still can't believe the way people pitched in to help the day the furniture arrived," I confided. "The delivery came early and I wasn't anywhere near ready for it."

"People around here believe in being neighborly," Annie said.

"I guess I was most surprised by *which* neighbors showed up. Jonah has always been ready to lend a hand, but two of the local cops? They were off duty, too."

"I think Steve Fleming likes you."

I choked on the sip of tea I'd just taken. "Oh, please! He thinks I'm a pain in the butt."

Steve, I thought, trying to decide whether or not the name suited him.

"One thing doesn't rule out the other." Annie helped myself to another cookie. "He's single, you know."

"And I'm sure there's a reason for that."

"I'm guessing it was Jack Ippolito who came with him." At my nod, she continued. "Now *he's* happily married with three kids, but he and Steve have been buddies since they were kids. They still spend a lot of time together on and off the job."

"Lila Jackson sent her assistant over. Eliot something."

"Carstairs."

"Steve and Jack seemed to know him."

"Well, I guess they should! He's been in trouble with the law often enough. No one's supposed to know the details because he's still a minor, but he was arrested for breaking into some of the camps in the area during the off season and stealing the liquor the owners were foolish enough to leave behind."

As a precaution, I set my cup and saucer on the coffee table. The way things were going, it seemed likely that Annie had more startling tidbits to share. I didn't want to take the chance I'd spit out my tea in response to the next one.

"He's a burglar?" I had difficulty keeping my voice level.

Annie grinned at me. "Not a very successful one by all accounts. Anyway, given his age, he was assigned to do community service instead of jail time. I was approached about taking him on at the animal shelter. I declined. My clinic is in the same building and so is my supply of veterinary medicines. I don't think young Eliot is any too bright. I couldn't take the chance that he might decide to help himself to some of the drugs I keep in stock."

"So Lila got him instead."

"Yes. As far as I know he's working out okay at the library. How did he get along with Steve and Jack?"

"They hassled him a bit, but in a good-natured way. I didn't get the sense that they were worried about him walking off with any cash or jewelry I might have left lying around."

"Somehow I don't picture you as the careless type," Annie said. "In fact, if you keep a lot of cash on hand, I'll bet you have a very secure hiding place for it."

I neither confirmed nor denied her guess. I reached for my cup again, took a long swallow of tea that was now lukewarm, and debated with myself whether to broach the subject of Aaron's enemies. Steve Fleming had been quick to shut down my suspicions, but then he had never put much stock in my theories to begin with. It was certainly possible I was wrong about everything, but if there was even the slightest chance I was correct in my thinking, I owed it to Aaron, and to myself, to keep asking questions.

"Let me ask you something, Annie. Have you ever heard any rumors of bad blood between Aaron Millard and Henny Horton?"

Annie peered thoughtfully at me over the rim of her teacup. "Aaron could be . . . crusty. He had strong opinions and he was set in his ways. That said, I don't recall any specific incidents between him and Henny."

"How about violent incidents in her past?" I asked.

"None I know of. Why?" She tucked a long strand of red hair behind one ear and sent me an inquisitive look.

Lucky hopped into my lap. I put aside my cup and focused on stroking the little cat's soft gray fur. "She's opinionated."

"Well, yes. Another of our local characters, just like Aaron was."

Unwilling to explain myself and have yet another person tell me I was letting my imagination run away with me, I spent the rest of Annie's visit talking about animals.

THE NEXT MORNING, LESS than one week before the grand opening of Veilleux Photography, I was doing a final count of matted but unframed prints of some of my favorite cat photographs when Wanda Newbury phoned to ask if I'd like to buy any of Aaron Millard's darkroom equipment.

"I thought you were going to hold an estate auction for the contents of the house."

"You saw the place," Wanda said. "There wasn't enough in it for more than a consignment to the local, small-time auctioneer, the one who'll sell you a trunk full of moldy books for a dollar on any given Saturday night."

"I don't really need more equipment. Aaron left a fully furnished darkroom behind here in the studio."

"Can you at least take a look and give me some idea what this stuff is worth? Maybe it'll do better in Uncle Henry's than in an auction if I know what to list as a price."

"Uncle Henry's?"

Wanda laughed. "I keep forgetting you're not from around here. You probably think eBay is the only way to get rid of your old junk."

"I don't know much about eBay, either. Who's Uncle Henry?"

"Not who. What. It's a weekly catalog of things people have to sell. You put in an ad, with your contact information, and chances are pretty good that someone will want what you're offering. You can sell your items, or you can offer to swap for something someone else is trying to get rid of."

Only in Maine, I thought.

Although it was true that I didn't need any more photographic equipment, and I certainly wasn't an expert on how much an old enlarger or a safelight might be worth, I agreed to meet Wanda at Aaron's house and take a closer look at what was there. An hour later, I was in the darkroom, inventorying its contents piece by piece and making my best guess about their value while Wanda, armed with a clipboard, took notes.

"You should dispose of the chemicals," I advised. "There isn't much in the way of photographic paper, but I can make you an offer on that. It's about the only thing I have a use for."

"Take it. Consider it payment for your help."

"Okay." I stood in the center of the small room, hands on my hips, contemplating what was there and what wasn't. "I still think it's odd."

"What?"

"There are no negatives. Aaron never did any digital photography. He used film, and that means there should be negatives as well as prints of his work. I didn't find a single negative in the darkroom at the studio, but it doesn't look like he took them with him when he closed up shop, either. As many years as he was in business, there should be thousands of them."

"Maybe he destroyed them." Catching sight of the expression on my face, Wanda waved off my objection before I could vocalize it. "Okay. Okay. I can see something like that would be considered sacrilege by a professional photographer. So where do you think they are?"

"I have no idea."

Wanda shook her head. "I've been through the whole house with a fine-tooth comb. If there had been a stockpile of negatives, I'd have found it."

Had Aaron really destroyed his life's work? I had to suppose he was discouraged when he went out of business, but he'd left behind all those albums. Why not just abandon the negatives at the studio, too?

As I turned away from the long counter by the sink, I reached for the small stack of boxes of photographic paper, none of them more than half-full. Because I was preoccupied with the mystery of the missing negatives, I failed to get a good grip. The top box, the lightest of the lot, slipped out of my grasp and landed upside down on the floor, spilling its contents.

With a sigh, I handed the other boxes to Wanda and knelt to pick up what I'd dropped. One of the sheets had slipped all the way underneath the counter. It was only after I'd retrieved it that I noticed what was sticking out from the tiny gap between the wall and the back of the sink. Reaching up, I caught hold of the corner—all that was showing—and gently tugged until an entire strip of negatives came free.

"Well, well," Wanda said. "What have we here?"

"Let's find out." Rising to my feet, I held the negatives up to the overhead light.

Images are always a bit difficult to make out when light and dark are reversed, but in this case there was no room for doubt about what we were seeing. Each tiny negative showed a variation of the same thing. A woman dressed in a skimpy negligee posed on a bed. The poses ranged from seductive to raunchy.

"Why, Aaron, you sly dog, you," Wanda murmured.

"I don't think he took these for himself." I squinted at the negatives in an attempt to identify the woman. "Some photographers specialize in what they call 'boudoir photography.' Women have sexy photos taken of themselves to give as presents to boyfriends or husbands. I don't think this was Aaron's usual line of work, but if he was strapped for cash . . . " I let my voice trail off, wondering what else Aaron Millard might have done to make ends meet.

With Wanda's permission, I took the strip of negatives home with me.

LATER THAT DAY, I MADE prints of each shot. I wasn't sure why. Eight-by-ten black-and-white glossies didn't tell me much more than the negatives had. I didn't recognize the woman posing so seductively on a bed that might, or might not, have been her own. There was nothing in Aaron's studio that matched and I hadn't seen anything like it in his house, either.

Had he gone to his client's home to take the boudoir photos? I wasn't sure if that made the concept more or less sleazy.

"Listen to me," I muttered under my breath. "Criticizing another photographer for shooting semi-nudes."

Most people would think just as little of me for some of the calendar shoots I've done. The film *Calendar Girls* inspired a lot of imitations.

I couldn't help but wonder how long ago these photos had been taken. These days, anyone with a little ingenuity and a selfie stick could accomplish the same thing without the bother or expense of hiring a pro. Come to think of it, I had no idea exactly when Aaron had actually closed up shop. A couple of years ago was pretty vague. Two? Three? Did it matter?

I wandered out of the darkroom, through the middle room, and into the front part of the studio. My gaze fell on the round table. It no longer held Aaron's photo albums, but the fact that he'd left them behind made the absence of negatives all the more inexplicable. If he wanted to erase every trace of his life's work, why not get rid of the albums, too?

Because, I thought, *the photographs in the albums were the height of respectability.* He'd been proud of them.

I walked to the front window and stared out at the electronics store/computer repair shop directly across the street. The curtains twitched in the apartment above, as if someone stood there, looking back at me. I couldn't make out the person's identity, or even be certain it was a person—cats and dogs look out of windows, too—but I lifted my hand and gave a little finger wave before turning away.

I had retreated into my tiny office, where I was still in the process of setting up a backup system of my own for my work, when another thought struck me with almost physical force. I dropped into my desk chair, staring at nothing, as I contemplated the possibility that it had been a set of negatives the burglar had been after. That would account for breaking into both Aaron's house and the studio.

I had no idea how much boudoir photography Aaron had done, but it made sense that not every recipient of such photographs would react the same way. What if one of the husbands or lovers had been furious that a photographer had seen what should have been reserved for his eyes alone?

It was time to get the entire sequence of events straight in my mind, and to do that I had to ask the right questions. I went upstairs, pausing only long enough for a brief cuddle with Lucky, before I collected a college-lined eight-by-ten tablet and a pen. Once I was settled on the sofa with those items, my laptop, and my cellphone, I called Annie Denton.

"I'm making a timeline," I said when she answered. "Do you know how long ago Millard Photography closed its doors?"

Her answer surprised me. He'd stuck it out until just over twelve months before my first visit to Waycross Springs.

"The place looked more and more run-down every time I visited him," Annie said, "but right up until the day he closed for good, he insisted on going to work six days a week year-round. Even after it became abundantly clear that very few people in town needed the services of a professional photographer, he made himself available. It was sad, really. He just couldn't keep up with the times." She hesitated. "I saw him at the food pantry more than once. I volunteer there sometimes. There's a lot of food insecurity in Maine. There's no shame in taking a handout, but after that, I tried to offer Aaron a meal I'd made myself when it was something like lasagna and I could say I'd made too much. I didn't want him to feel like a charity case. You could tell he hated the idea that anyone would pity him."

Guilt nearly swamped me. How could I have been so blind to his reduced circumstances? There had been plenty of clues right in front of me.

"I should have paid more attention," I said aloud. "I might have found a way to help him out."

"You bought his business. I'd say that was a big help."

It was on the tip of my tongue to ask Annie if she had any idea what Aaron might have done with the money from the sale, but she was already speaking again.

"He even made an effort to decorate the studio for the holidays that last year," she said. "He strung lights, the old-fashioned kind that aren't considered particularly safe these days, and put a wreath on the front door. I remember I started to poke my head in and tell him how nice it looked, but he was with someone and the tension in the air was thick enough to cut with the proverbial knife."

I sat up straighter. "As if they'd been quarreling?"

"Sounded that way. I didn't stick around."

Did you recognize the other person?"

"Sorry. No. Just a bulky shape with its back to me."

"How long after that did Aaron go out of business?"

In the long silence that followed, Lucky hopped into my lap and demanded attention. Absently, I stroked her with one hand while clutching my pen so tightly in the other that my knuckles showed white. Even before Annie answered, I had a feeling I knew what she was going to say.

"It was just a few weeks later."

Now it was my turn to hesitate. "I found some negatives," I said slowly. "It looks like Aaron was shooting pictures of scantily clad women in seductive poses." I explained about boudoir photography and then cut to the chase. "Is it possible *that's* what the man was so upset about?"

"You think someone took a gift of sexy pictures the wrong way?"

"Maybe. What if that's what the burglar was after when he searched Aaron's house and my building?"

"I think you're letting your imagination run away with you," Annie said.

Why, I wondered, had I expected her reaction to be any different than anyone else's?

"I've got to get back to work," Annie said. "Do you want me to come over later? You sound like you need someone to talk to."

"That's okay. I have some work to do myself." And I had Lucky to use as a sounding board. One thing about cats—they never try to tell you that your ideas are nonsense.

After I disconnected the call, I looked down at the lined tablet on my lap. I'd not only written "angry stranger" on the page, I'd circled it repeatedly, bearing down so hard with my pen that I'd nearly torn the paper. With a sigh, I removed the top sheet and started over, making a list that ended up containing very few actual dates. It did include all the assorted conflicts I'd been told about: Aaron and Jonah; Aaron and Henny; Aaron and the chief of police; Aaron and the mysterious stranger. I could date that one to December. Directly beneath it I wrote: *January of last year: Aaron goes out of business.*

Then what? I thought for a moment before writing anything on the next line. I didn't have an exact date, but given Lila's clothing, it had been winter. The same winter Aaron closed up shop? Or this past winter, just before I made an offer for the studio? Had Aaron been desperate enough to take a commission to spy on Lila for her ex-husband, then changed his mind when the money from the pending sale freed him from the need to take George's money?

Thinking of Lila reminded me of the library and young Eliot, the juvenile offender. When had he been caught breaking into camps? More importantly, when had he stopped? Or had he? Could *Eliot* have been the burglar Aaron fought with?

Still pondering that possibility, I completed my timeline by adding my own movements. I'd passed through Waycross Springs on my way between two shoots in February, spotted the "for sale" sign in the window of Millard's Photography, and been intrigued enough to contact Aaron. It hadn't taken us long to agree on the terms of the sale. Then it had just been a matter of finishing up a few commissions before returning in April to sign the papers. Four days later, he'd been struck and killed by a hit-and-run driver who had yet to be identified, let alone arrested.

I flipped to the next page and made a new list, this one consisting of anyone who might possibly have had it in for Aaron Millard:

Henny Horton

Brent Gilroy

Lila's ex, George

angry stranger

Eliot Carstairs

I could see one or two of them as burglars, but did any of them have a reason to kill?

Then, too, it was possible the hit-and-run driver and the burglar were two separate people.

Setting aside the legal pad, I stood and stretched. I wandered over to the front window and glanced outside just in time to see the curtains twitch at the window directly across from my apartment. A cold chill ran up my spine. I retreated so rapidly that I nearly tripped over the cat. From a safe distance, I tried to see more, but now that I was watching, nothing moved.

Paranoid much? But I couldn't shake the feeling that someone in that room had been spying on me.

I know what rational people think of conspiracy theorists. I share that opinion.

I'd heard that big life changes could be stressful. Surely that was all it was. Moving to a new place. Setting up a new business. Aaron's death. All those things took a toll on the nerves.

Lucky stropped herself against my legs. A glance at the cat was all it took to bring me back to reality. There was a hit-and-run driver. There was a burglar. But maybe I'd had the right idea earlier. What if the two were not the same? There are such things as coincidences.

I glanced again at the window on the other side of Main Street. I had no idea who lived there, but I was undoubtedly making too much of a few curtain twitches. Of course the neighbors were interested in me. I was a newcomer in town. I had a nosy neighbor with nothing better to do, maybe even a shut-in. I'd have to make it a point to find out who lived there, but that was not my highest priority. Neither was catching criminals.

My *job* was to open my business and make a place for myself in my new hometown. It was time I started focusing on that.

"What do you think, Lucky?" I asked. "Should I host an open house for the business or just unlock the door and hope people come in to see what I've done to the place?"

If the turnout for Aaron's celebration of life were any indication, folks would stop by out of sheer curiosity. Whether they'd have any need for my services remained to be seen.

THE FOLLOWING MORNING, I was putting the finishing touches on a calendar I'd designed to give away as an advertisement for Veilleux Photography when someone knocked at the back door. I gave a start and turned to see Steve Fleming smiling in at me through the glass. My heart rate settled a little when I realized he was not in uniform, but that left me wondering what it was he wanted with me.

Only one way to find out, I thought, and eased out of the desk chair to cross the short distance between it and the exit and open the door.

"Hey," he said, stepping inside.

"Hey, yourself. What's up?"

He held out a bakery box. "Rumor has it you've been working too hard. I thought you could use a break."

"You brought me food?"

"That's a matter of opinion. I brought you doughnuts. Now if you could see your way clear to provide some coffee to go with them . . ."

Discombobulated was the word that best described how I felt, but I waved him toward the stairs. "We'll have to go up to the kitchen for that. I haven't gotten around to buying a separate coffeemaker for the office."

"Not a hardship," he assured me, but his gaze fell on my computer monitor before he could set foot on the first step. "Hey, that's Lucky!"

"Multiple Luckys. I'm putting together some promo material."

He stepped closer to the screen. "I'd heard you did calendar art, but I had no idea the results were this fancy."

Fourteen pages were displayed, from the front cover through all twelve months to the back, where there was also a photograph of the front of my building and the brand new sign that said Veilleux Photography in fancy script. A sidebar listed my hours and some of the photographic services I offered.

"I'm still fiddling with it."

"You're good," he said.

"Don't sound so surprised."

He chuckled and followed me up the stairs. "I hear the grand opening is set for next week."

"I may have a soft opening over the weekend."

"Soft opening?" he asked.

I managed a smile. "Unlock the door and hang out the OPEN sign. See who wanders in."

"Ah."

Lucky appeared two seconds after I opened the apartment door, prancing toward us with bright eyes and an upright tail, clearly hoping someone would replenish the food in her bowl, or at the least provide her with a cat treat. Then she noticed the doughnuts.

"Shameless beggar," I scolded her after I filled two mugs with coffee and carried them to the table. Looking hopeful, Lucky had her front paw on Steve's knee.

"I don't think a bite of one of the plain ones will hurt her." He offered it up without waiting to hear my opinion.

"It isn't necessary to bribe my cat," I informed him. "Lucky already likes you."

"Yeah? Good. How about you?" He turned the bakery box around so that I could see the selection he'd brought.

My mouth watered. I have a decided weakness for Boston Creme doughnuts with their chocolate frosting and yummy filling and there were two of them in the box. There were also two plain and two powdered and they were still warm.

"Did Henny make these?"

"Henny is a genius with breads and cakes and cookies, but for these you need to go to a little specialty shop on the outskirts of Waycross Springs. I'm surprised you haven't already discovered it."

"I've been kind of busy." I bit into the doughnut and closed my eyes with the pure bliss of its taste. "Oh, this is delicious."

"Always do my best to please a woman," Steve said.

My eyes popped open to stare at him.

"That didn't come out quite right."

I waved off any further apology but snagged the second Boston Creme and plunked it down on my plate before he could get his hands on it.

He grinned and pinched another small section off one of the plain doughnuts for Lucky.

"I should be bringing you doughnuts," I said, "to thank you for your help the other day."

"We had pizza."

"*Henny* sent that."

He shrugged and reached for one of the powdered doughnuts.

I ran a finger around the rim of my coffee mug. This seemed like a golden opportunity to find out more about several of the townspeople, but wasn't sure I wanted *Officer* Steve Fleming to know why I was interested in these particular individuals.

"Is this your day off?" I asked.

"Long weekend."

"It's Tuesday."

"Cops don't exactly work normal schedules." He polished off his coffee and got up to refill his mug.

"So instead of sleeping late, you decided to bring me doughnuts?" I was missing something, but I wasn't sure what it was.

"Can't a new acquaintance stop by just to see how you're doing? Things have been pretty hectic for you ever since you arrived."

"You could say that, what with Aaron Millard dying and all."

He winced. "I didn't mean to remind you of that, or your break-in. I just meant you've been busy fixing up the place, and moving into this apartment, and getting ready to open the studio. That's a lot."

"Have the police made any progress in finding out who ran Aaron down?"

My blunt question didn't seem to surprise him, but neither did it prompt him to share. "I can't talk about an ongoing investigation."

I sighed. "Well, at least it *is* ongoing. I was afraid the case had been closed."

"Give me a break. This may be a small town, but we're not inept at our jobs."

"What about the chief?"

"What about him?" His expression turned wary.

"Does *he* know what he's doing? Because I have to tell you that I haven't been too impressed with him so far, and I know Aaron Millard wasn't."

"If Millard had reported that break-in, it would have been investigated."

Where before Steve's eyes had been full of good humor, now they'd gone cold. There was a tension to him that hadn't been there before. It was almost enough to make me regret pushing him for answers. Almost.

I drew in a deep breath. "I think I know what the burglar was after."

"You *think*, or you *know*?"

"I have an educated guess. Two, actually."

He'd lost all interest in both coffee and doughnuts, sliding his plate to one side so he could make space on the table for the small spiral notebook he'd taken out of his shirt pocket. I kept one wary eye on him and the other on Lucky, who had hopped up onto one of the empty chairs. The cat took advantage of Steve's distraction to snag the last bite of powdered doughnut. She took off with it before I could stop her. Chasing her seemed like a waste of time, especially when I finally had Steve's full attention.

First I told him about the film I'd found in one of Aaron's cameras. I didn't name Lila, but I did stress that there might be an abusive ex-husband in the picture. That he'd hired Aaron to take the photographs made more sense than Aaron as a stalker.

"I think Aaron took the assignment because he desperately needed money, but he was too ethical to complete the job once he realized his client's intentions."

"So this guy, what? Broke into Aaron's house and your apartment looking for those photos? Sounds to me like he already knew where his ex-wife was. Otherwise how would he have known to hire Aaron?"

"He tried to kill her so she wouldn't leave him. Maybe he ran Aaron down in a fit of rage because Aaron quit on him."

"You said you had two guesses about the would-be burglar's identity. What's the other one?"

"Aaron apparently had a sideline he didn't advertise. Come with me."

I led him into the living room and retrieved the envelope in which I'd put the prints I'd made from the negatives I'd found in Aaron's at-home darkroom. After giving Steve a brief account of how I'd come by them, I handed them over.

He shuffled through the photos, surprised into a low whistle.

"The deal with these is that they're intended for the eyes of one man only, although obviously the photographer also sees them. They're a far cry from being pornographic. Some would even call them artistic. By the same token, they aren't anything the subject would want to find posted on the Internet. The thing is, if this set exists, then Aaron probably did other similar photo shoots."

I told him about the tense interaction Annie had witnessed between Aaron and an unidentified man. Although I hadn't felt comfortable giving him Lila's name, I had no such qualms when it came to Annie. I felt certain she wouldn't mind repeating her observations to Steve.

"I'm not saying it was that man who broke in looking for negatives," I added, "but someone's husband might have."

"Not hers," Steve indicated the woman in the photograph he held.

"You know who she is?"

"Don't you?"

I shook my head.

He grinned. "Valentine Veilleux, meet Natalie Gilroy."

"Gilroy? As in—?"

"Yeah. That's my boss's wife. She's married to the chief of police," he added, just in case I missed the significance. As if I could!

The woman was young. Much younger than Brent Gilroy. "How long ago do you suppose these were taken?"

Fleming shrugged.

"A decade? A year? A few weeks?"

"Not a decade. She's only twenty-five."

"Good friends with her, are you?"

His laugh was wry. "Hardly. The boss keeps her under wraps. He—"

I studied his face, saw the frown form, followed by a pained expression. "What are you thinking?" I asked.

"Better you don't know." Abruptly, he rose and headed for the door.

THAT EVENING I WENT for a walk to clear the cobwebs out of my brain. I ended up standing in front of Aaron's house, staring at the FOR SALE sign the bank had put up.

"That didn't take long," I muttered, and jumped at the sound of a snort from behind me.

A woman who looked vaguely familiar stood there, a leash attached to an elderly collie gripped tightly in one hand. "He wouldn't have been surprised," she said.

"Aaron? Why not?"

"Because he didn't have one good thing to say about that bank after he figured out he'd probably outlast the payments he got from them for that reverse mortgage. Switched his social security deposits to their competition, even though that meant he had to cadge a ride from me or one of his other neighbors to get there if he wanted to cash a check."

"Wait a minute. Are you telling me he had a checking account at another bank?"

"Sure. The one out on the highway. Drove him there myself more than once. I'm Addie Clermont," she said. "I was at that shindig you hosted for Aaron but we didn't get a chance to talk, what with all the other folks around."

"You're a neighbor?" I asked, shaking the extended hand.

"That's right. For more years than I want to own to."

"Did you happen to take Aaron to the bank one day last month?"

"Sure did. He was in a very good mood that day." She grinned. "Just sold his studio to you for a nice chunk of change."

I grinned back at her and thanked her for the information. Then I pulled out my cellphone and called Wanda.

She picked me up on her way to the bank. Before I had time to buckle my seatbelt, she hit me with the news that Aaron's request for cash had been bogus. "Seems he simply wanted to hassle the bank because of that blasted reverse mortgage. He took a cashier's check."

"And marched it straight to the other bank in town?"

"Looks that way. We're about to find out."

Wanda's standing as Aaron's executor meant she got prompt answers. Aaron had opened a checking account for the automatic deposits of his social security checks and he'd made a very large deposit on the day he sold his studio to me. He'd also rented a safe deposit box in which he'd stored the few records he'd bothered to keep.

"Looks like he'd been maxing out his cards for living expenses," Wanda said after she looked over the paperwork. "He used a large part of the money he got from you to pay them off, but there's still a nice legacy left over for the food pantry."

With one mystery solved, I was more eager than ever to have answers to the rest of my questions. When I got home, I phoned Lila.

"I was just wondering if you'd thought any more about those photos Aaron took," I said when she answered. "I really think you should tell the police about them."

Ten minutes later I disconnected and crossed another suspect off my list.

Lila had contacted an old friend in her former hometown and found out that her ex was in jail and had been for months. He might have hired Aaron, but he hadn't been in any position to follow up. Best of all, he wouldn't be for another decade or more.

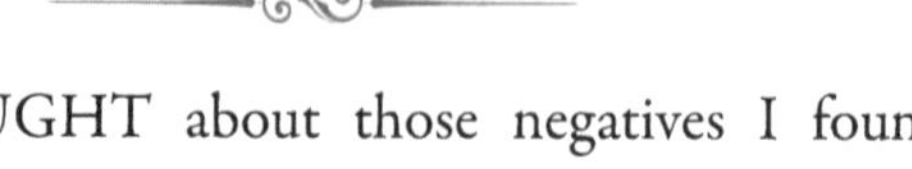

THE MORE I THOUGHT about those negatives I found, the more uncomfortable it made me to hang on to them. I could have destroyed them, but that didn't set right with me. So, bright and early on Thursday morning, the day after Wanda and Lila solved two of the minor mysteries surrounding Aaron Millard, I found myself on the Gilroys' porch. I rang the doorbell and waited. I had about decided no one was at home when the door opened just a crack. The safety chain was still on.

"Who are you? What do you want?" Natalie Gilroy's words were hard to catch but I couldn't miss the tremble in her voice.

"I'm Valentine Veilleux, Mrs. Gilroy. The photographer who bought Aaron Millard's studio."

I heard a sharp intake of breath.

"Could I come in for a minute, Mrs. Gilroy? I have something that belongs to you."

"Oh, God!" The door slammed shut, but a moment later, the chain off, it opened wide enough to let me slip inside.

She didn't look much like her photograph. Older, yes, but also aged in a way that had nothing to do with the passage of time. There were deep shadows under her eyes and she seemed to shrink into herself as I stared at her. "Are you all right?"

"Yes. No." She made a helpless gesture with one hand. "It doesn't matter. What did you bring? Did you find the negatives?"

"Have . . . have you been looking for them?"

Although the light was poor in the hallway where we stood, it was bright enough to show me fresh bruises on her bare forearms. It didn't take much of a leap to realize the woman was terrified, or that the obvious cause had to be her husband's temper.

Struggling to keep my voice level, I said, "I guess your husband didn't react the way you hoped when you had those photos taken."

"Oh, God," she said again. "He pitched a fit when he realized Aaron had seen me in my nightclothes. I don't know what he did, but he must have put the fear of God into that old man. The next thing I heard, he'd closed up shop and wasn't taking pictures of anybody anymore."

Had it been Gilroy who Annie saw? That seemed likely.

"Was it your husband who broke into Aaron's house and my studio?" I asked. "Was he looking for the negatives?"

"I don't *know*," she wailed.

I had trouble with the idea myself. Why wait so long to look for them? Besides, it seemed too big a coincidence that the negatives from Natalie's photo shoot were the only ones I'd found. They'd obviously been left behind by accident.

"Do you think he'd have hurt Aaron?" I remembered the bruises I'd seen on Aaron, the result of tangling with his burglar.

"I don't have any idea how far he'd go." Despite her denial, Natalie didn't seem surprised by my question. "*Do* you have the negatives? Please, if you do, give them to me. I just want this nightmare to be over."

Unable to resist the pleading note in her voice, I produced them.

I can't explain why I didn't also give her the prints I'd made.

WHEN I GOT HOME, I phoned Steve Fleming and asked him to meet me at my apartment as soon as possible. He arrived within the hour. I'd just finished filling him in on what I'd learned from Wanda, Lila, and Natalie when I happened to glance out the window. I was just in time to see a flash of light from the apartment across the street. My first thought was that it came from a camera lens, but as I stared at the spot the curtains twitched and gave me a better view.

"Someone's watching us with binoculars."

Steve was at my side in an instant, but he wasn't fast enough. Whoever it was realized he'd been seen and retreated into the interior of the apartment.

"Which window?"

When I pointed it out, a grim expression came over his face.

"You know who lives there?"

"I do. Come on."

Five minutes later we were standing at the top of a steep flight of stairs and Steve was banging on a wooden door.

"Open up. Police."

"I don't have to talk to you without my mother here."

The voice seemed familiar. "Is that—?"

"Eliot, I'm not kidding around. Open the da—"

The teenager who'd helped move furniture into my apartment stood in the doorway, a defiant look on his face. "I didn't do nothin'."

Steve pushed past him, pulling me inside with him. He waited until Eliot closed the door behind us before he leveled his accusation. "You were spying on Ms. Veilleux. I want to know why."

"I didn't take anything."

"No one is saying that you did," I interjected before Steve could speak again. "But you have been watching me. I saw you at least twice." There had been a previous curtain twitch, and that time someone had ducked into an alley when he saw me looking his way.

"Yeah. Ok. So what?" He hesitated so long I could almost hear the gears turning as he tried to come up with an excuse. "Maybe . . . maybe I think you're hot."

"Get real." He was so obviously throwing out the first possibility that came to mind that I had to fight a smile.

"Eliot, you're on thin ice here. Just level with us, okay?" Changing tactics, Steve erased every hint of threat from his voice. "We aren't trying to get you into trouble." He put one hand on the boy's shoulder.

I watched Eliot's face work. For a second, I thought he might be about to cry, but he pulled it together and almost managed a nonchalant shrug. "You guys need to get your stories straight."

"I beg your pardon?"

"You cops. Do you want me keeping an eye on her and reporting back or not?"

That statement baffled me, but Steve caught on. "Who? Who pressured you to spy on her? Was it Chief Gilroy?"

"Well, yeah. Who else? He said I had to. Part of my community service."

"And I'll bet he told you not to mention this to anyone else, right?"

Eliot sent him a wary look. "Did I screw up?"

Steve sighed. "No. I think I'm the one who did that. Okay. Here's the deal. You stay put and don't talk to anyone till you hear from me. Not even the chief. Especially not the chief. Got that?"

Eliot nodded, looking as confused as I felt.

I waited until we were back across the street to demand answers.

"I don't have any," Steve insisted. "Not yet. Will you make me the same promise Eliot just did?"

"Shut up and sit tight?" I let just the tiniest hint of sarcasm creep into my voice."

"That would be a big help," he said.

"Are you going to talk to the chief? Do you think he's the one who broke into Aaron's house and my building? If he was looking for those negatives, he—"

"No use speculating until I check on something. I'll be back before you know it. Don't go anywhere," he added as he left.

He didn't see the mock salute I sent after him.

TOO RESTLESS TO HANG around in my apartment, I retreated to the darkroom to develop the roll of film I'd shot over the last few days with one of Aaron's cameras. I was anxious to see the results.

I had just reached the point where the negatives needed to go into the stop bath when the darkroom door flew open and the overhead light flashed on. I turned, ready to flay a strip of skin off whoever had ignored my DO NOT ENTER—DEVELOPING IN PROGRESS sign, but the words died in my throat when I recognized the chief of police.

Brent Gilroy looked like a man on the verge of apoplexy. I took a step away from him, but there wasn't much room to maneuver and he was blocking the only exit. I swallowed hard, suddenly very much afraid of what the man might do next.

"You gave the negatives to my wife," Gilroy shouted.

I managed a nod. What on earth was he so upset about? I'd have thought he'd be glad to know where they were. If he was the one who'd broken into Aaron's house and my studio and he'd been looking for those negatives, then he ought to be happy to finally have them in his possession.

"How'd you recognize her, huh?"

"What?" I was truly at a loss.

"Don't play dumb with me. You can't tell diddly-squat from a negative. You printed copies."

"They're in my bag. Upstairs. I'll get them."

"Are there more copies?"

"No. Of course not."

"I don't believe you. Maybe you were planning to use them to blackmail me."

"Are you out of your mind?" The words were out before I could stop them. Appalled, I snapped my mouth shut. Of course he wasn't quite sane. That went without saying.

"I want the truth."

"I've told you—" I broke off as he produced a gun.

He pointed it at me. "The truth," he repeated. "Where did you find the negatives? Have you had them all this time?"

Knees weak, I braced myself with one hand against the table that held my developing equipment. "The negatives had slipped behind the work station in Aaron's home darkroom. He couldn't have known they were there."

But even as I said it, I wondered. It seemed too great a coincidence that the only negatives left behind were the very ones Gilroy wanted.

Gilroy swore under his breath. "I didn't believe him the first time he said he couldn't find the negatives. Made him give me every one he had."

"*You* took the rest of Aaron's negatives?"

"Back before he closed the studio. Destroyed them all, just to make certain. I never should have believed him when he said there weren't any more."

With that gun still leveled at me, I struggled to make sense of what I was hearing. "I thought you were the one who burgled Aaron's house," I blurted.

"You thought right." He took a threatening step toward me.

I held my ground, but only because I had no place to retreat. *Keep him talking,* I thought. *If he's talking, he's not shooting.*

"What made you think the negatives hadn't been destroyed?"

"He was boasting about coming into money. Figured he was getting ready to blackmail me."

Okay, I thought. *That's some leap in logic. He really does have a screw loose.*

Then again, knowing Aaron, it was entirely possible the old man had encouraged him in his misconception just for the fun of it. Or out of revenge for destroying the other negatives. Then, when he'd caught Gilroy searching his house, he'd started to have second thoughts. Had the warning he'd meant to give me concerned the possibility that the chief might try to break into the studio next? If that was the case, had Gilroy known of Aaron's intention? Had he quarreled with Aaron on the day he died? Had *Gilroy* been the one who'd run Aaron down?

I felt myself blanch.

Gilroy's eyes narrowed to slits. "Figured it out, did you?"

The hand holding the gun shook a little, but if he fired it, I wouldn't be able to avoid being hit. In desperation, I reached for the nearest throwable object, grabbed hold of it, and flung it in his direction. At the same time, I dropped into a crouch, curled myself into a ball, and covered my head with my arms.

The sound of a gun firing in the close quarters of the darkroom nearly deafened me, but Gilroy's howls of pain still penetrated the ringing in my ears. The container I'd thrown at him had not just spoiled his aim, causing the bullet to land harmlessly in the ceiling. It had contained the stop bath solution. Corrosive glacial acetic acid had splashed into his face and eyes.

I'd just kicked the gun out of the way and was attempting to render first aid when Steve Fleming burst into the darkroom. He had read Chief Gilroy his rights, arresting him for murdering Aaron Millard and attempting to murder me well before the ambulance arrived.

"How did you know?" I asked as we watched the EMTs lead Gilroy away.

"About the hit-and-run?"

I nodded. "He didn't actually confess to that. There's no proof."

His smile was grim. "Oh, yes, there is. That's what I went to check on just now. We have solid evidence from the lab. It was the chief's cruiser that struck Aaron down."

Although I couldn't take any pleasure from being right about the intent behind the hit-and-run, and I wasn't looking forward to having to rehash it all at Gilroy's trial, I was glad all the questions about Aaron's death had finally been answered. "The worst is over," I said aloud.

"It is," Steve said, sliding one arm around my waist. The look he sent me was both flirtatious and hopeful. "And the best could be about to begin. What do you say to a celebratory meal at Aphrodite's?"

I smiled up at him, letting him see the same possibilities in my eyes.

"I say that sounds like a good place to start."

About the Author

Kaitlyn Dunnett is the pseudonym used by Kathy Lynn Emerson for the Liss MacCrimmon Mysteries and the Deadly Edits Mysteries. Under those names and others she has had sixty-four books traditionally published in several genres and has independently published others, including *I Kill People for a Living: A Collection of Essays by a Writer of Cozy Mysteries.* A link to a complete list of her books can be found at www.KathyLynnEmerson.com.

www.ingramcontent.com/pod-product-compliance
Ingram Content Group UK Ltd.
Pitfield, Milton Keynes, MK11 3LW, UK
UKHW041852190726
13854UKWH00002B/861